Mastering The Art of Female Cookery

Cyan LeBlanc

Undertaker Books

Copyright © 2024 by Cyan LeBlanc

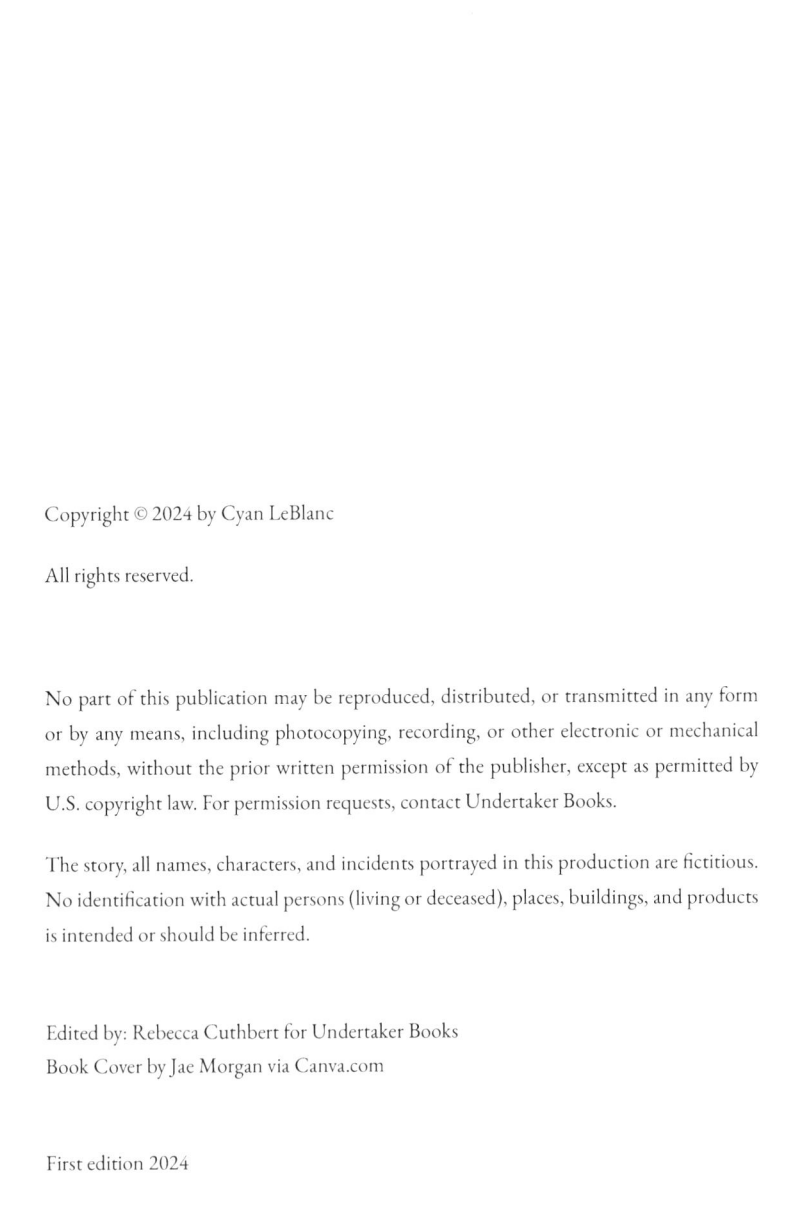

All rights reserved.

No part of this publication may be reproduced, distributed, or transmitted in any form or by any means, including photocopying, recording, or other electronic or mechanical methods, without the prior written permission of the publisher, except as permitted by U.S. copyright law. For permission requests, contact Undertaker Books.

The story, all names, characters, and incidents portrayed in this production are fictitious. No identification with actual persons (living or deceased), places, buildings, and products is intended or should be inferred.

Edited by: Rebecca Cuthbert for Undertaker Books
Book Cover by Jae Morgan via Canva.com

First edition 2024

Reader Advisories

This book is a satirical rendering of memoirs, autobiographies, and cookbooks blended with extreme horror. While its intention is dark humor, it does contain sexually explicit material and considerable violence.

Please be ready for gore, cannibalism, murder, assault, and other possible triggers that are standard within the slasher horror and extreme horror subgenres.

DISCLAIMER #1: If you are in any way against reading about the natural sexual development of teenage identity, including masturbation, please skip chapters 3 and 4. Avoiding these two chapters will not hinder the process of the story.

DISCLAIMER #2: Because this book is satire, the author makes no claim that the recipes are correct or that they will make a delicious meal. They were found online, modified for humor and narrative purpose, and are untested.

Introduction

I've been pigeon-holed by my morning writers' group. When I first wrote *Dying to Meat You* and *The Taste of Women*, they all laughed and rolled their eyes at me and my dive into the horror genre world. While I had other horror novels planned, every time I opened my mouth regarding new books, there was this inherent joke that each one would be another cannibal book.

The Taste of Women exceeded my expectations. I never thought my Sapphic readers would embrace the horror world with me and enjoy the idea of lesbian cannibals as much as they did. Reviews were very positive. Two or three times there were jokes made about how to cook human flesh.

When I laughed about the reviews to my morning group, they suggested that I write a cannibal cookbook. Well, at least one of them did. Mayra Luria, this book is for you.

I took them seriously, and did it. This was probably the easiest book for me to write. Why? I have no clue. I busted out the story in less than a month, then took the rest of the time to find recipes online that worked within the confines of the story and added them in. This book felt like a dish; I had all the ingredients and I just needed to mix and blend them all together for a novel.

The story follows another person in the cannibal world I had already written about in my previous two horror books. *The Taste of Women* talks about a disease that plagued a woman who needed to eat human meat in order to survive. In creating a cannibal universe, this is the story of a young girl whose family is murdered at the hands of cannibals; much like Valerie in *The Taste of Women*, whose lover also became a victim of possibly the same clan. This story touches more on how a woman becomes infected, though it does not talk about where the disease originated. That topic I've planned for another book. Yes, there are more cannibals coming your way—because I've been pigeon-holed into being "the lesbian cannibal writer."

Please remember, this type of female cannibalism is fiction. If you want to run out, bite someone, and tear off a hunk of flesh, be my guest, but there is nothing sophisticated in eating a woman in that manner. Women are meant to be savored.

So please, allow me, if you will, to take you on this journey of ***Mastering The Art of Female Cookery***.

Chapter 1

June 29, 1977. The memory of this day haunts my every sleep. It was my seventh birthday and my family and I were on our way to visit my aunt in St Louis, Missouri from Albuquerque, New Mexico. Summer vacation and all the time in the world. My father took the scenic route, traveling up Route 66, where we stopped at all the roadside attractions to take snapshots. We had just passed Oklahoma City, driving north in our Pontiac Grand Safari toward Tulsa when my father decided it was about time to call it a night. He didn't want to stay in a big city because of the high prices, so wanted to look for a motel somewhere in between those two towns.

My 15-year-old sister Marie and I were in the back seat asleep when our father turned off the infamous route. When the car hit a bump in the road, we jolted awake with sleepy eyes to see if we'd arrived yet. I looked out the window and saw nothing but darkness and the rain dripping down the window in front of me.

"Fuck!" my father, Jack, yelled, banging on the steering wheel. "I think I missed the fork. There's nothing out here."

I giggled at my father's curse words, especially when my mother, Celeste, reprimanded him for using them in front of "the children." It wasn't like we hadn't heard them before, but Mother was prim and proper. Unlike me, a scabby-kneed tomboy who hated dresses and lace. Marie got the girly genes while I was the "son" my father always wanted. I played sports, rode my bike fast and hard, and wrestled with him while Marie wore makeup and tied up the phone most evenings, chatting with her boyfriend, Chip.

The rain continued to pour around us, and the car's headlights did nothing to brighten the road. Windows fogged with our combined breath, and Father wiped his hand on the windshield to clear a better view. Any time things didn't go right, my parents argued. This was one of those times.

"Jack, slow down and turn on your brights," Mother demanded of him.

"I'm not going fast. Calm down!" he replied as he fumbled with the dial to the left of the wheel.

When my father tilted his head toward the instrument panel, unable to find the dial, Mother hollered, "Watch the road!"

"I am!"

Finally, the bright headlights illuminated the road in front of us and, out of nowhere, they cast upon the figure of a small child, a little girl around my age, standing in the middle of the road. My father stomped on the brakes, throwing all of us forward as the burning rubber screeched, sending our station wagon spinning in circles.

I screamed. Marie screamed. So did Mother. When the car finally came to a halt, we all opened our eyes to find we were alive and well. No one was hurt, which my father confirmed.

The car seemed to have missed the stray child, who we could not find when Father jumped out to inspect any damage. My father was correct when he said, "We would have felt her body if we had hit her."

No one felt anything, though Marie and I were adamant that my father had killed this child, who might have been dead in a ditch somewhere. To this day, I am not at all convinced that he didn't; although we had not heard the horrific crunching sound of running over a living creature as it scampered, trying to escape death by metal and rubber and exhaust fumes. Only once in my lifetime had I experienced that blood-racing thud under my car–the sound of some feral creature losing its life. When it happened, I was too afraid to check what I had hit while being in an unsavory neighborhood in the middle of the night. Instead, I pressed the gas pedal slowly and heard the bone crushing cracks as the car lunged over whatever it was I left in the road. Not my proudest moment, to say the least.

But that night, on a dark Oklahoma road, after deeming the car was drivable and we were all fine, Father returned to the vehicle and we proceeded on our way. He wanted to get off the single-lane road and back on to the highway. It was my crying, Marie's whining, and Mother bickering that caused him to pull off to the side of the road and yell at everyone to shut up. He was lost, turned around, and didn't know which direction was north. With the rain still coming down, that was all we heard: the *ting* of large droplets hitting the metal roof as he inched along.

We came upon a small, off-beat town with a gas station, a motel with maybe two or three rooms, and a diner, whose sign had one letter burned out. The letter "O" was dark, barely noticeable on the neon sign where the letters should have read *Hello Kitchen*. That was exactly what this would become for me. Hell Kitchen.

By this point, the water fell from the sky like a tidal wave. Father had to pull over. The defroster had given out and the wipers couldn't keep up. We pulled into the parking lot of the diner and on the count of three, we all rushed from the vehicle and blasted through the entrance to avoid as much of the storm as we could.

Like wet dogs, we shook the water from our clothes and hair at the entrance of this quaint place.

A burly woman with her hair in a bun and a pig nose greeted us. "It's sure a mess out there. Come on in, we'll fix you up something to warm your cockles."

At seven, I didn't know what that meant, but any time I hear that word, I transport back to June 29, 1977. She sat us in the booth closest to the front door. There were only two booths and three tables in this small diner. Perhaps being so far off the main highway, it was only frequented by locals. Two other customers were in the diner at the time we came in. A woman, early to mid-twenties; she had dirty blonde hair and looked more like Farrah than Farrah herself. The other woman sat at the small counter across from the cash register. I could only see her from behind, but I knew she was a woman from what happened later.

While the pig lady left us to bring glasses of water, the flicker of neon came through the window behind me and my father. It seemed to burn into the table like a branding iron. I traced the backward red letters with my finger while we waited. When she returned with the water, I reached for it, but my father grasped my wrist. He wiped the glass rim with a napkin before allowing me to drink.

The waitress pulled out a pad of paper and a pen. "We don't have a big menu here. We're just a small town, much like a family. Kind of sit around and eat the same thing. Tonight, I made Beef Bourguignon, which is just a fancy way of saying beef stew. If y'all want something else, I might be able to whip you up a hamburger or something."

I recognized her attention being drawn to my mother and sister, who sat opposite my father and me. Her nose wiggled like a piggy's sniffing the air. "Oh, that isn't necessary," my mother said, her usual polite self "Is it, Jack?"

"No, not for me, but Cora, what about you? Do you want a hamburger or this...beef stew she made?"

I glanced at my mother, then shrugged because she gave me that look she always did when she wanted me to agree with her. "Whatever you guys are having."

"Perfect. I'll wrestle you up a few bowls." Pig lady stepped away from our table and got lost behind a swinging door in the back.

Next to that saloon door was another one with a restroom sign on it. Marie had asked if she could use it, so she and Mother scooted out of the booth. Mother held out her hand for me. Despite not needing to go, Father stood so I could follow along with them.

The small, cramped room contained only two stalls and one sink. It wasn't the cleanest bathroom I'd seen, but it certainly wasn't the dirtiest, either. Leaning against the wall with my hands behind my back, I waited for them to go first. Shortly after they entered the stalls, the Farrah lady walked in behind us.

As soon as she entered, we exchanged smiles. I was so captivated by her hair that I nearly missed my mother's question. "Cora, are you still in here?"

"Yes, Mommy," I replied, observing the woman taking slow, deep breaths at the sink. It brought back memories of visiting the doctor, when he'd press the stethoscope against my back and tell me to take a big breath in.

Her chest rose high and fell, as if trying to sniff out a strange smell. At seven years old, this act seemed strange to me. I looked toward the stalls and saw Mother's and Maria's panties, pulled down between their ankles, both showing bloody pads stuck to the fabric. Farrah glanced back at me through the mirror, licking her lips. The moisture made them gleam like the shine of pink lip gloss.

When they finally exited their stalls, Farrah entered one of them while they washed their hands. Mother said, "You should try to use the restroom, Cora. Knowing you, we'll go sit down, and then you'll need to go. So, just do it now."

She wasn't mistaken. I always seemed to follow that pattern. I complied with my mother's request and entered the other stall, just sitting there and listening to Farrah's heavy breathing. Looking back, I'd say she was panting. Amidst my mother and Marie's conversation and the sink's running water, I doubt they heard it.

However, I watched her foot bounce as her breath quickened. My heart raced, almost trying to match its rhythm. I'm not sure what drove me, but I reached my hand under the stall. Farrah grabbed it, squeezing my little fingers, and then her foot ceased its bounce. Her breath calmed, and she let go. It was then, finally, that I pushed out a couple of drops of urine, just as the woman flushed and exited the stall.

"Are you almost finished in there?" Marie hollered.

I glanced under the stall to see Farrah's feet next to my sister's. They were close. Very close. My mother's feet were nowhere in sight. Quickly, I pulled up my pants and pushed out of the stall. My sister's eyes widened, her skin turning a pasty shade, like glue. At that moment, Farrah looked over her shoulder at me and left the room. Marie stood frozen, as if rigor mortis had seized her limbs.

"Are you okay?" I asked Marie.

"Go back to the table. I'll be out in a minute." She remained almost motionless, but I followed her instructions, anyway.

As I left, I quickly glanced back at Farrah's booth before moving on, crawling under the table past my father's legs and slinking into my seat. Moments passed, and Marie reappeared from behind the door, still looking shocked.

Beef Bourguignon awaited us on the table, triggering memories of the pot roast and gravy my mother used to prepare. The aroma made me momentarily forget about Marie's withdrawn state. I dug in, and, oh my goodness, the taste was unlike anything I'd ever experienced. It was certainly not like Mother's pot roast. My taste buds awakened like a roaring engine in a diesel truck. All my senses went into overdrive as I devoured the meal.

"My goodness, looks like someone here was super hungry," my father remarked, noticing how quickly I wolfed down my portion while he had barely taken a few bites.

Since Marie hardly touched her meal, I asked if I could have some of hers. She pushed the plate across the table, wrinkling her nose at it. I happily indulged in her leftovers until my mother pulled the plate away. "That's enough. You'll end up with a bellyache in the middle of the night if you keep eating."

When the rain finally eased, my father decided it was time to head out again. However, my mother admitted she'd rather call it a night and resume the journey in the morning; I could tell she was still shaken by the sight of the child in the middle of the road–there and gone. After Father agreed to cross the road and rent a room at the shady motel, we all got up from the booth. I was still riding the high from whatever ecstasy—be it a drug or euphoria—I had just tasted. I sprinted to the door, making my way to the car. Father naturally bolted after me. That left Mother and Marie to settle the bill in the diner.

Pig Lady stood by the window near the door as I burst through it. When my father followed me out, we heard the bolt of the diner door locking behind him. He yelled, and I initially thought he directed it at me. When I turned back, though, I saw him pounding his fists on the door.

"Hey. What's going on? Let me in."

The words grew more angry, more urgent, as he resorted to using swear words he typically avoided in front of us. I hurried to the door, peeking in from beneath my father's towering figure. And that's when I saw Pig Lady, Farrah, and three other women strip the clothes from my mother's and sister's bodies and sink their teeth into their bloody female parts, starting with their spread legs, then ripping their nipples off their breasts like tearing pieces away from a raspberry fruit roll-up.

My family's screams pierced the closed door and the glass panes. I was stiff with horror. My eyes never once blinked as Pig Lady raised a cleaver over her head and brought it down right on to Marie's neck. Blood sprayed the glass in front of me as her round head, blonde curls still attached, rolled toward the door. It stopped when it hit the glass. Her wide, lifeless eyes stared at me, as if silently pleading for help. I reached out and touched the glass, as if hoping for some miraculous intervention.

Their limbs, once battling, now lay still in pools of crimson on the floor. Mother had ceased her struggle against the attackers. A tear escaped her eye, her arm extending out in one last attempt for us to aid her. Then, everything fell silent.

"Get in the car! Get in the car!" Father yelled at me.

I obeyed, watching as he hurried around the back of the building, desperately searching for a way inside to rescue them.

With the car doors locked, I pressed my back against the car, clinging to it as if I were a magnet latched onto the steel frame. The horror inside consumed me, similar to the scary movies my father watched late on Saturdays—films he wouldn't allow me to see, yet I couldn't resist hiding behind the sofa to watch. If this situation was anything like those movies, I knew the ending: we were all going to die.

Beef Bourguignon

You're probably wondering what happened to this seven-year-old child who was alone in the middle of the night somewhere in Oklahoma, right? We'll get to that in the next chapter of my life. For now, I'd like to discuss this mind-blowing, life-changing dish I tasted. It wasn't until high school that I started to dabble in cooking. More out of a necessity than anything else.[1]

I'm leaping forward in my story to share a recipe that holds a significant place in my culinary journey. This dish marked a turning point for me, encouraging me to expand my cooking horizons. It was a reminder that our tastes as humans have evolved far beyond primitive instincts. While I've developed an appreciation for more exotic flavors, I still hold a deep love for the simplicity of green chilis, spices, salt, and other delightful ingredients that enhance flavors.

That bloody desert diner has haunted me throughout my life, yet I've never been able to pinpoint its exact location, where the tragic events of 1977 occurred. Over the years, I've tried to retrace my steps along the lengthy stretch of road between Oklahoma City and Tulsa, but the diner has remained elusive. I'm not entirely sure why I've subjected myself to this ongoing torment, trying to revisit what feels like a recurring nightmare. However, someday, I hope to finally locate it. In the meantime, the memory of that "stew" has lingered, shaping my dining preferences. Whenever I dined out, I ordered beef stew, pot roast, or similar dishes. At seven, I couldn't recall the Pig Lady's words "Beef Bourguignon" to save my life.

I scoured through cookbooks relentlessly until, one day, a word triggered a lightbulb moment. This was the dish! The memory of sitting at the diner with Farrah in front of me, the backward "Hell Kitchen" glowing on the table, surged back. It transported me to that moment when the Pig Lady said, "Beef Bourguignon, which is just a fancy way of saying beef stew."

My first attempt at this recipe was a disaster. It tasted so terrible that I ended up vomiting at the kitchen table. Let's just say stomach bile and beef stew weren't a winning combination. I must have tried 50 different versions of the same dish, attempting to replicate it until I finally figured out the missing ingredient. Human flesh. A woman, to be more exact.

Over the years, I've dedicated numerous hours in my kitchen aiming to perfect it, striving to recreate an exact replica of what my seven-year-old memory recalled. This involved determining the precise cut of meat to use. Similar to a cow, I discovered I could derive the closest match from the fleshy part under the arms, but not the breast meat. The goal is to find that flavorful back fat, which keeps its juiciness and contributes the ideal amount of oils when simmering.

Ingredients

1/2 pound bacon-style belly meat (page: 19), sliced

1 tablespoon olive oil

3 pounds lean stewing meat (cut into approximately 2" chunks)

1 carrot, sliced (coarse chopped)

1 onion, sliced (not diced or chopped)

1/4 teaspoon pepper

1 teaspoon salt

2 tablespoon flour

3 cups full-bodied red wine

2-3 cups beef stock (page: 23)

1 tablespoon tomato paste

2 cloves garlic, smashed

1/2 teaspoon thyme

1 crumbled bay leaf (optional)

For the brown-braised onions

1/2 bag frozen white pearl onions, defrosted and patted dry

1 1/2 tablespoon butter

1 tablespoon olive oil

1/2 cup beef stock

Salt and pepper

For the sautéed mushrooms

1 pound mushrooms, quartered

4 tablespoon butter

Salt and pepper

Instructions

- Gather and prepare your ingredients prior to cooking. Chop the bacon, chop the beef (that juicy back meat), chop the veggies, smash the garlic. If you prepare your ingredients, "mise en place" it will help things go smoothly once you fire up the stove.

- Preheat oven to 450 degrees.

- Arrange the beef chunks in a single layer on a tray lined with paper towels, almost like putting together a human puzzle. Use additional paper towels to thoroughly pat the beef dry. Damp beef will not brown properly. This is important... No one likes wet meat.

- In a large Dutch oven, heat the olive oil over medium heat. Add the human bacon and cook until it is browned and has released most of its fat. Use a slotted spoon to remove the bacon, leaving the fat in the pan for later.

- Over medium-high heat, brown the cubed meat in the bacon fat for two minutes on each side. Don't overcrowd the pan. Even a dead person doesn't like to feel like a sardine. You will do this multiple times until you finish all the meat. The meat should develop a nice, caramelized brown on the surface. Turn the beef to brown on all sides, then remove with a slotted spoon and set aside. *If your beef is not browning properly, it is either due to the heat not being high enough; the pan being over-crowded (which lowers the heat of the bacon fat), or the beef being too wet.

- Add the carrots and onions to the pan of bacon fat. Cook for a few minutes until they develop a golden-brown color, then pour out the excess bacon fat, leaving the veggies in the pan. *I like to keep the fat for reheating for later. The more you save, the less you have to find when hunting for your human meat.

- Add the bacon and beef back into the pan with the veggies. Toss with a little salt and pepper.

- Sprinkle flour over the mixture and toss again.

- Place the pan, uncovered, on the middle rack of the preheated oven for four minutes. After the initial four minutes, toss the mixture and then cook for an additional four minutes.

- Remove the pan from the oven and reduce the heat to 325 degrees.

- Add the wine, beef stock, tomato paste, garlic, and thyme. *Add enough beef stock to barely cover the beef. With the wine, I recommend a dry wine, such as a Merlot or Pinot

Noir.

- Bring to a simmer on top of the stove.

- Cover the pan and place it in the oven. Cook, covered, for about three hours. *Adjust the temperature slightly, if necessary, so that the liquid maintains a gentle simmer throughout the cooking time. While the beef is cooking, prepare the onions and mushrooms.

For the onions

- Heat the butter and oil in a sauté pan over medium heat. Add the onions and cook for about 10 minutes, occasionally shaking the pan to allow the onions to roll around in the pan and brown on all sides.

- Add the beef stock. Bring to a simmer, then lower the heat.

- Cover and simmer slowly for about 15-20 minutes. Toward the end of the cooking time, most of the liquid should have evaporated and formed a brown glaze around the onions.

- Season with salt and pepper, and set aside.

For the mushrooms

- Heat the butter in a sauté pan over medium-high heat. Add the mushrooms.

- Cook for about 10 minutes, stirring frequently. The mushrooms will appear to absorb the melted butter, but will release the butter and their own liquid. As the liquid evaporates, the mushrooms will acquire a golden-brown color.

- Season with salt and pepper, then set aside.

Return to the main dish

- Once the beef has finished cooking, carefully pour the mixture through a strainer. Allow the sauce to collect in a large measuring cup or glass bowl.

- Pick out the carrots and onions, and discard. Return the beef and bacon to the Dutch oven.

- Arrange the brown-braised onions and sautéed mushrooms over the beef.

- Allow the sauce to rest for a few minutes. The excess fat will rise to the surface as it rests. Use a spoon to collect and discard the excess fat. Don't you wish you could do that with your own body, just skim off your fat? Oh, well... Keep repeating the process until you have discarded a significant amount of the excess fat. *You should have about 2-2 1/2 cups of sauce. If you have much more than this, pour the sauce into a small saucepan and simmer uncovered until it's reduced. It should be thick enough to lightly coat the back of a spoon. Taste and adjust the seasoning with salt and pepper, as desired.

- Pour the sauce over the beef, mushrooms, and onions.

You can serve this dish over your choice of accompaniment: boiled potatoes, hot-buttered noodles, or even alongside de-boned fingers stuffed with cream cheese. Alternatively, it's delicious on its own. This meal reheats beautifully. Just bring it to a gentle simmer on the stovetop for a few minutes until all components are heated through.

---

1. At puberty, my growth spurt went in reverse. By the time I figured out what I needed to survive, I looked like a sack of bones.

Bacon

As with almost everything I eat, most of the protein elements I process myself. Since I cannot actually call up my local farm and request human "bacon" or human "ham" per se, I've had to take creativity to the next level to cure my own meats.

In this section, I'll be teaching you how to create your own bacon-style meat, perfect as a substitute for any recipe that typically calls for pork-sourced bacon.

1. Choose the right belly.

If there is an opportunity to pick and choose your human, I recommend locating a chubby person. This poses a few challenges if you are not strong. You may have to recruit a second person to move your overweight victim, but this is the most ideal cut of meat for "pork" products. This is where I find men to be a better choice, as well. Women will be on the fattier side while a man with a beer gut will have more lean meat on the cut. By the way, a full pork belly weighs 10 to 12 pounds.

2. Remove the meat and skin.

First, make a cut at the groin. Slice from one side of the pelvis to the other. Next, slice along the side from just under the breast area to the hip. Repeat on the other side. From here, you will lift the flap of meat away from the torso, like opening a window into the person's abdomen. You can either filet the meat off the skin or, more easily, slice just under the breast to have a square of belly fat.

To remove the skin, start at one corner and use a sharp, slender knife to separate the skin from the meat, angling the knife blade toward the skin.

Note: Do not discard the human skin. Save it for later. You can grill it over a medium flame on both sides (start belly side down) until crisp and golden brown to make crackling crisp bits of skin to fold into pulled or shredded meats. Or you can deep fry it in oil to make chicharrones, which is great on beans or greens. But, my favorite way to use human skin is like a tortilla.

3. Prepare the cure.

The core ingredients are salt, sugar, and pepper. To explore a diverse and nuanced flavor spectrum, experiment with different sources and proportions of these ingredients: white sugar, brown sugar, maple sugar, or even freeze-dried cane sugar juice. For pepper, consider using ground or cracked black pepper, or even hot pepper flakes. You can also enhance the mix by incorporating juniper berries and other aromatic spices. When preparing the cure, mix the ingredients by hand, especially if using brown sugar, to ensure you break any lumps up with your fingers.

4. Cure the pork belly.

Arrange the belly on a rimmed baking sheet. Season and rub both sides with the cure from above. Place the belly in a large, sturdy, resealable plastic bag in a roasting pan on the bottom shelf of your refrigerator. Keep it there for five days, remembering to turn it over each day. This step is crucial. As the cure dehydrates the meat, liquid will collect in the bag. This is an expected part of the process, similar to brining.

5. Rinse and dry the belly.

Transfer it to a colander or strainer and thoroughly rinse both sides with cold water to eliminate the excess salt. Then, blot the belly dry and position it, uncovered, on a wire rack atop a baking sheet, placing it on the bottom shelf of your refrigerator. Allow it to dry for at least four hours, or preferably overnight, turning it once or twice. This process aids in forming a "pellicle," an outer skin that feels papery and dry, perfect for the smoke to adhere to. Achieving this exterior skin is essential for the bronzed surface that makes bacon look undeniably delicious.

6. Smoke the bacon.

If you have accepted your cannibalism, a smoker will be your best friend. Set up your smoker according to the manufacturer's instructions and preheat it to 175 degrees. If you're using a charcoal smoker, the temperature will fluctuate between 160 and 180 degrees. That's okay. If using an electric or gas smoker, you can set it at 175 degrees.

For smoking, use hickory, apple, cherry, or other preferred hardwood (or blend of woods). I find mesquite to be too strong, personally. Depending on your type of smoker, you'll use chunks, chips, sawdust, or pellets. The smoking time will range between two to three hours. What you are looking for is an internal temperature of 150 degrees.

7. Chill and rest the bacon.

Allow the bacon to cool to room temperature on a wire rack placed over a baking sheet. Once cooled, tightly wrap it in plastic wrap and refrigerate for a minimum of four hours, or preferably overnight. This process helps set the flavor and texture. When refrigerated, the bacon will stay fresh for at least five days. If frozen, you can store it for several months.

8. Slicing and cooking.

When becoming a serious meat eater, I highly recommend investing in a few essential items. One of these is a meat slicer. I suggest investing in a professional-grade slicer upfront. This initial investment will save you money in the long term and provide a wider range of options for deli-style cuts.

Beef & Chicken Stock

Do you know how many recipes need beef or chicken stock or broth? When I first started cooking, I tried the shortcut of using animal stocks when a recipe called for it, but I found it left a bitter aftertaste in the dish. Some people might not object to the flavor, especially when new to cannibalism. Or even if you are hosting your first dinner party with individuals who have not yet been converted into cannibals. By mixing meats, you are introducing them to a new cuisine without overloading their palates.

If you are fully turned and feeding a growing family, it's wise not to waste any part of this body, including the bones sitting in your deep freeze. For that, I like to take off as much of the viable meat as possible, then save the bones for stock. But don't shave off every nugget of meat. You need that extra on these bones because meat equals flavor.

For both beef and chicken stock, the recipe is much the same. I have learned to divide up the body into sections. Arms and legs make a better chicken stock, while backs and necks are great for beef stock. You will need to break or cut the bones into pieces if you are using a standard 12- or 16-quart pot. *Marrow bones are the cross section of the pelvic bone.

Ingredients

5 large bones (back and neck preferably) plus one pelvic bone for richness

1 carrot, unpeeled, cut in half

1/2 onion (white or yellow), peeled and cut in half

2 tomatoes, cut into quarters (keep seeds in)

1/2 tablespoon coriander seeds

1 tablespoon apple cider vinegar

1/2 tablespoon black peppercorns

1 celery stem, cut in half or thirds with leaves

2 bay leaves, fresh (or 1 dried)

2 thyme sprigs (or 1/2 teaspoon dried leaves)

12 parsley sprigs, if you have it but not essential

3 quarts water, cold tap water

Instructions

Roast bones:

- Preheat oven to 420 degrees.

- Spread bones out across two baking trays. Roast for one hour, turning at 30 minutes, or until very well browned.

- Drain and discard excess fat, if any.

- Place bones into a large stock pot.

Deglaze the baking trays:
- Place tray on stove, turning burner to medium. Add 3/4 cup water. When it simmers, start scraping the tray. The drippings on the tray will loosen and dissolve into the liquid.

- After removing most of the drippings from the base, scrape all the liquid into the pot. Repeat with other tray.

Simmer stock:
- Add remaining ingredients into the pot. Start with 1/3 water, then squish the bones etc down to fit snugly in the pot. Add more water if needed, to just cover the bones. The ingredients will collapse a bit as stock cooks. The water quantity depends on the shape of bone and pot.

- Bring to a boil on medium-high, then turn down to low so it's simmering ever so gently with only a small bubble bursting now and then.

- Scoop off any surface scum using a ladle and discard.

- Simmer for eight hours on very low, no lid. Liquid level

should be reduced to around four quarts for all. If not, just reduce after straining.

Other methods:

Slow cooker for eight to 10 hours on low. Reduce after straining to 1.5 qt.

Strain & finish:

- Fish out most bones. Strain stock with the remaining vegetables through a fine mesh colander or strainer over a large pot or bowl. Leave the strainer for a few minutes to let it drip.

- Set stock pot or bowl in the sink filled with a few inches of cold water. Leave stock to cool for around an hour and 15 minutes, changing the water every 20 minutes or so as it gets warm.

Measure stock volume:

- Pour stock into a vessel to measure volume. It should be between 1.3 to 1.7 quarts. If it's much more, reduce on the stove, otherwise the stock flavor will be too weak.

- Refrigerate stock. When fat has solidified on the surface, carefully scrape off with a large spoon and discard. You should have 1.25 to 1.5 quarts remaining.

- The stock is now ready to use. This stock is equivalent in strength to store-bought stock, so we can use it 1:1 in any recipe calling for beef stock.

NOTE: Homemade stock is unsalted whereas store-bought stock is salted. Add 1/4 teaspoon salt for every one cup homemade beef stock to match the salt level of store-bought low sodium beef stock.

To use:

Cold stock has a jellied consistency. It takes barely a minute to turn liquid on a medium-high stove, or microwave. You can also just add it in jelly form straight into dishes, but sometimes you may need to liquify it to measure.

Storage:

Seven days in the fridge, or three months in the freezer. I like to portion into usable quantities such as one cup or two cups, label, and then freeze in containers.

Chapter 2

The last thing a seven-year-old girl expects is to witness her entire family being slaughtered before her eyes. Yet, on June 29, 1977, that horrifying event occurred. Initially, shock overtook me more than fear. By the car, which wasn't far from the door's entrance, I couldn't look away from the diner. My sister's decapitated head lay on the floor, her eyes fixed on me. Her expression mirrored the horror in my own eyes. It wasn't until Farrah walked to the door and picked up my sister's head that I finally shifted my gaze away from Marie. Farrah and I locked eyes. Strangely, amidst the horror, a sense of amazement lingered, burying my fear beneath layers of skin and flesh.

After Farrah walked away from the window, all I could see were feet darting around the room, leaving bloody footprints in their wake. Someone dragged the bodies across the tiled floor, leaving behind a trail of red streaks, innards, and carnage. With the rain beating down on me and my back pressed against the car's frame, I felt utterly alone.

When I finally summoned the nerve to pry my little body from the safety of the car, I noticed a dog chained to a post off to the side of the parking lot. I pushed away and walked carefully toward it, which made it spring to life. Its barking startled me at first, sending me butt-first into a puddle of mud. I couldn't seem to catch my footing enough to pull myself up. Just then, I felt the arm of someone assisting me.

The person was a little girl, a year or two older than me, also covered in mud with her hair flattened by the rain. If it hadn't been wet, it might have formed wavy, brown curls. A surge of panic coursed through my tiny body, making me tremble. I wanted to break away from her, but her hand in mine eased the growing fear.

"Are you going to kill me, too?" I asked, a stutter in my voice.

"No. They don't want you. You're too little. Just a girl, not a woman."

I peeked around the edge of the building to a small patio sheltered by an awning. There, I saw my father's body lying on the ground, blood forming a stream on the cement. I wanted to run to him as tears bubbled in my eyes but this girl grabbed my hand, keeping me with her and dragging me toward the back.

As I heard her voice again, I turned my head. "What's your name? I'm Sadie."

My trembling voice managed, "Cora. Are you one of them?" Not that I knew what *they* were, other than murderers. At seven, nothing made sense.

"Not yet. Do you wanna come to my house and watch some television?" Sadie asked, as if there was nothing peculiar about the diner being the site of a horrific event, killing three innocent people.

Once more, my undeveloped mind could only grasp two things: my family was dead, and we had been en route to my aunt's house in St. Louis—that was where I should go. "I have to go see my aunt. She lives in St. Louis. I should go now."

"You don't have to leave in the middle of the night. Stay. Leave tomorrow during the day."

"I'm not allowed to go off with strangers."

"I'm not strange. I'm Sadie. You're Cora."

She tugged my arm and led me to her small, shack-like home—wooden planked walls and rickety steps guiding us to the open front door. The screen creaked as Sadie pushed it open. Inside, a flickering television set with metal antenna rabbit ears struggled for reception. A brown and orange tweed-upholstered sofa faced the TV, sitting atop an avocado-colored carpet, worn from constant use. *Charlie's Angels* played on the screen, startling me with Farrah's presence, but that was the real actress. Frightened by a loud bang against the door frame, I glanced behind me, finding no one there. Sadie grasped my arm and guided me down the musty hallway to her room, where she had an assortment of toys—nothing new, all used and worn.

We sat in the center of the floor, each holding Barbie dolls as we played, or more so Sadie played. I sat on the floor clutching the doll with ratty blonde hair, not being able to move much or even say much. When my nerves finally allowed me to join in, I reached for the Ken doll off to the side.

Sadie grabbed the doll from my hand and tossed it back in the pile of unused toys. "Barbie doesn't like Ken. She likes other Barbies. And they put their faces right there like dessert."

There was a very... let's say, innocent explanation of how lesbianism worked with two dolls, one of which was turned upside down. I see that now, looking back as an adult, but what my child brain told me at that time was that women eating other women's private parts was a way to die. Seven-year-old Cora had just seen that with her own eyes. I didn't want to play that game anymore, where bad things happened. Back home, Chester was mean to his rabbits. I couldn't watch that, so I wasn't going to watch Sadie do mean things to Barbie. Instead, I left the room and returned to the living room, where I watched Farrah chasing bad guys.

During the evening, I dozed off on the sofa; only to awaken when the screen door opened. My eyes shot wide open at the sight of the fake Farrah coming through it, but I immediately squeezed them shut so hard that I saw red splotches on the backs of my eyelids. I wanted her to think I was dead, so I tensed my body and didn't move. Eventually, I fell asleep again.

When I awoke once more, the sun had risen and the aroma of food drifted into my little pug nose. Without paying attention to my surroundings, I followed the scent of something delicious and stood in the doorway between the living room and the kitchen. As Farrah turned around, her sudden movement startled me. I spun around, sprinted back into the living room, and then out the front door. By the time I reached the yard, Farrah had already bounded down the stairs. My feet slipped on a patch of wet soil, causing me to tumble. When I glanced back to see how close she was, I scooted on my rump, trying to escape, but she was faster and soon I cowered on the ground.

I curled into myself and screamed, "Don't eat me!"

"I am not going to eat you. Now, simmer down and come on. Let's get some breakfast," Farrah said as she grabbed my arm and scooped me up like I was weightless.

Despite still believing she wanted to make a meal out of me, I didn't protest too much about returning to the house, where Sadie was now in the living room with a bowl of cereal in front of the television.

"Are you gonna run off again? Do I need to lock us inside?" Farrah asked, holding the door. All I could do was shake my head. "Good. Now, we should probably get you cleaned up, and then you can have some cereal with Sadie."

I hesitated as she traipsed down the hallway toward the bathroom. At the door, she waved me forward. "Come on, now." By the time I reached the bathroom, Farrah had the water running in the bath. She asked, "Do you take baths or showers?"

At that point in my life, baths were for nighttime relaxation and preparing for sleep. In the mornings, we took showers when we were on the go. It seemed like a simple answer, yet I couldn't stammer out the words.

She nodded. "Here's what I'll do. I'll leave the water running. If you want a shower, turn the middle knob. If you want a bath, just put the plug in the drain. I'll pull out some clean clothes for you to wear."

Once I was alone, I turned the middle knob and started the shower. I peeled off my muddy clothes and climbed into the tub, closing the yellow plastic curtain with flowers on it. Looking back at that moment, in that house, it wouldn't have screamed "serial killer," especially with a bottle of green apple-scented shampoo in the corner, which I used. The door opened once and closed again during my shower. When I finished and turned off the faucet, I found a clean pair of corduroy pants and a striped shirt.

When I stepped out of the room, I caught the savory scent of sizzling meat in a frying pan, mixed with a familiar aroma of simmering sauce, much like when my mother made spaghetti. I followed my nose to the kitchen once again. At the table, Farrah sat with a pile of scrambled eggs with spinach and slices of what looked like ham. Across from her was a bowl of cereal and a jug of milk.

"Don't you clean up well. You can take the bowl into the living room with Sadie, or join me at the table. Your choice," Farrah said, then she stabbed a piece of the pinkish meat and stuffed it into her mouth.

There was something about Farrah, now that I saw her as less intimidating, that was kind. Almost mothering, but she was too young to be a mother and too old to be a kid. With a pull of the chair, I joined her at the table but hadn't reached for the fruity and frosted circles in the bowl.

"Can I have what you're eating?" I asked.

"I can make you eggs, but nothing else."

I glanced at her plate again, analyzing it, silently questioning why I had to eat something else. When my eyes met hers, she shook her head with a faint tilt downward and said, "Just eat the cereal. It's better for you."

There was no protest as I poured milk over the contents of my bowl and shoveled spoonful after spoonful into my mouth. For some odd reason, my stomach seemed like an endless pit. When I emptied my bowl, she offered me seconds and thirds, until I drained the box of its last loop.

That's when Farrah finally said more. "Sadie doesn't have a lot of friends around here. Would you like to stay? Live here with us?"

My little undeveloped brain didn't take long to answer–didn't realize her invitation was a threat, that it was less question and more command. For a moment, I'd even forgotten my family was dead and gone. "No, I have to go to St. Louis to see my aunt. She's waiting for us to arrive, and then she's going to take us to see the big arch."

Her eyes, which 20 seconds before seemed hopeful and bright, were now tinged with sadness as my words came across the table. With that, she pressed her palms onto the table and lifted herself up. She said nothing as she reached across to take my bowl and her plate to the sink and tossed them in. Much like my mother when I said the wrong thing, she appeared angry with me. So, I did what I always did and walked away.

Giving a wave to Sadie, I stepped out the door, walked down the stairs, and into the dirt of the yard, careful not to slip into the muddy puddles. The house was behind the diner, across a back parking lot. When my stride hit the back patio of the diner, where I had seen my father's body the previous night, it was gone. So was the bloody river. I crossed along the side of the building to the front, where our family's station wagon no longer sat. It was gone too.

The events hadn't really sunk in yet, but not seeing the car struck me, and for a moment I was crushed by the thought that they'd left me behind. Tears streamed down my face as I stood where the vehicle once was, looking at the diner sign which read "Hello Kitchen" during the day.

The voice from behind me said, "I'll take you to Tulsa and put you on a bus to St. Louis."

I didn't turn around, but I knew the voice to be Farrah's. A few moments later, a white Buick Skyhawk pulled up in front of the diner with Farrah behind the wheel. The drive from wherever we were to Tulsa took what seemed like an eternity. She said nothing the entire trip. No radio. No conversation. I stared out the window, feeling a mindless, numbing sensation take over me, as I didn't know what would become of me without my family.

At the bus terminal, Farrah walked up to the counter and purchased a bus ticket for her "niece," who was going to visit her aunt in St. Louis. She paid for it using money from my father's wallet. Then she led me to the benches in front of my stop.

She squatted in front of me. "Now, when you get to St. Louis, walk around for a while, then find someone who works there. Tell them you are lost and your aunt never came to pick you up. They will call her, and I'm sure she will come get you. Do you understand?"

I nodded, still choosing not to say anything to her because I didn't know how to explain what I had just lived through, what I had seen. Even when I told Mother about Chester and his rabbits, it was said that I was making up stories to get other people in trouble. Mother insisted that I didn't tattle on anyone.

"Cora, I'm sorry for what you saw. One day, you might understand, but I really hope that you never have to live like this." She squeezed my little fingers in a caring way, much like Mother did when the doctor gave me a shot. Then she let go and stood up. "Be safe, little one."

When Farrah disappeared back inside the terminal, I felt lost and abandoned. With no mother, father, or sister, I had no one to guide me and reassure me that life would be fine. My heart ached as much as a child's could, and tears poured down my face, drenching my shirt. I longed for the security of someone holding my hand, so I leaped from the bench and ran into the terminal.

"Farrah!" I hollered. She wasn't anywhere. Vanished. Gone. And that is when I stopped speaking.

Green Eggs and Ham

Sam, I am not. Maybe at that time in my life, I wouldn't have liked what was on Farrah's plate. The green eggs were nothing more than spinach combined with scrambled eggs, and a couple of slices of what I have learned wasn't ham at all.

But it wasn't a member of my family on her plate. What I came to learn later is that there are necessary processes for specific types of meat consumption; it's essential for some meats to undergo a drying or curing phase to avoid a messy appearance on the plate. It typically takes four to 10 days to brine the meat properly, resulting in a juicy and flavorful ham. My family had not even been deceased for 24 hours.

The green eggs and ham recipe in this chapter is structured into two distinct parts. First, we'll explore the brining process for the meat, transforming it into a ham-like consistency. Following that, I'll provide you with a delightful recipe for spinach-infused eggs.

Ingredients

12 ounces kosher salt

10 ounces brown sugar

3 whole cloves

2 tablespoons crushed peppercorns

2 tablespoons coriander seeds (lightly toasted)

2 tablespoons fennel seeds

2 teaspoons ground mace

2 tablespoons chili flakes (optional)

1 teaspoon ground bay leaf

1 tablespoon mustard seeds (lightly toasted)

1 tablespoon oregano leaves

1 cinnamon stick (whole)

Instructions

- As with any brine, pickling spices are optional. If any of the above are not to your liking, leave them out. If using coriander and/or mustard seeds, lightly toast in a clean pan over low heat. Combine all ingredients in a large pan.

- Add room temperature water and set on a low heat. Stir until all sugar and salt have dissolved. Allow to cool completely.

Step One: Choose your cut of meat

While butchers traditionally make ham from the hind leg or shoulder of pork, using the thigh yields better results. If you cut at the knee and at the groin, you have a nice shank. Ideally, find someone with minimal fat and muscle. For this, women are better options. An average-size woman provides the optimal amount of fat-to-meat ratio.

For beginners, I suggest starting with slicing the top portion of the thigh rather than attempting to handle the entire leg. Mastering the fundamental steps and comprehending the underlying principles will make the subsequent process of preparing an entire leg less intimidating and you will be more likely to succeed. Aim for about four to six pounds of meat. Make sure you accurately weigh your meat before you start the next steps, as it's important for steps two and three.

Step Two: Prepare your brine.

How much brine you make depends on how big your piece of meat is. A general rule is you need to make enough brine to fully submerge your ham in its container and about 25% extra for pumping.

Step Three: Inject your meat

When creating a ham-style piece of meat, it's crucial to inject it with your brine to ensure thorough curing. This step is significant when dealing with cuts containing bones. Using a two ounce brine injector, get the brine as deep as possible, ensuring even distribution throughout the meat. Improper curing may cause portions of the meat not to cure adequately, causing them to turn gray. Although still usable, these areas will resemble roast rather than cured ham.

Your pump rate is 25%. If your meat weighs four pounds, then you need to inject it with approximately 17 ounces of brine.

Step Four: Cure your meat

Once you've injected your thigh meat thoroughly, place it in the remaining brine in your container of choice and store in the refrigerator. Ensure you fully submerge the meat. Curing takes five to seven days.

As a general rule of thumb, allow one day per pound of meat. For large cuts or full thighs, cure for a maximum of eight days.

What happens if you cure for longer? The salt, cure, and pickling spices will further penetrate the meat. Usually, the end product will be overly salty, so that's why I recommend sticking to the time frames above.

Step Five: Rinse and soak

After the curing process, remove your meat and thoroughly rinse it under a cold running tap, ensuring to remove all excess salt and spices. After this, soak your meat in room temperature water for two hours to further remove excess saltiness and cure.

Step Six: Equalize and form the pellicle

Place the meat on a plate uncovered inside your refrigerator for 24 hours. Two things occur during this time. The remaining cure and salt should equalize throughout the meat, resulting in a less salty and more even-tasting final product. Also, your meat will form a "pellicle," an exterior, tacky sheen that will appear on the surface of your meat. The pellicle will help your meat absorb a smoky flavor when it comes time for smoking.

*Note: this sixth step is optional. If you don't have time, or simply can't wait to eat some delicious thigh meat, dive in. You can eat it cold, or you can cook your human ham to your liking. I enjoy having it smoked with apple and maple chips. You can also use cherry, pear, plum, pecan, hickory, or peach wood.

Green Eggs

The eggs are the simplest part of this dish, as you can buy all the ingredients from a store. I always recommend saving any drippings when rendering meat, like making bacon-style meat, as these fats can be valuable. They are not only convenient but can also save you money by eliminating the need for extra oils or fats. This makes items like fried eggs an essential part of your sustenance. Anytime you can cook with human fat, this bodes well for your cannibal diet.

Instructions

- Crack eight eggs into a blender and add two cups of baby spinach.

- Blend until the spinach is completely incorporated, and it looks like a green smoothie. As much as this will look gross, it's a fun concoction for children.

- Pour eggs into a large nonstick pan on medium-high heat.

- Use a silicone spatula to gently scrape up the eggs as they cook, pushing them to the outside of the pan, and letting the uncooked portions run toward the center.

- When most of the eggs are still just slightly wet, sprinkle with salt and pepper. With one more gentle scrape and stir everything, remove them from the pan.

- Serve a scoop of green eggs with a side of warm ham.

Notes: Be cautious with the heat setting; high temperatures can cause dry, burnt eggs, especially when blending the spinach in. Nobody wants overcooked eggs. The recipe suggests cooking on medium-high heat, but for gas burners, opt for medium or medium-low.

Adjust the amount of spinach as desired; this recipe is quite versatile. You can add up to one loose cup of baby spinach per egg, or even use less spinach than stated in the recipe. For extra creamy eggs, sprinkle in some grated Parmesan when adding salt and pepper. Finally, savor your meal, but remember the ham!

Chapter 3

St. Louis posed some challenges when I first arrived. When the bus pulled into the terminal, I sat on the bus, not moving. It wasn't until the driver came up to me at told me it was my stop. I got off as instructed but I didn't interact with anyone like Farrah told me to do. I couldn't. I didn't really know how to tell someone my family had been eaten by strange women and one of them stuck me on a bus. So, I sat. Then used the bathroom. Then sat again.

Half the day went by before a man in a captain's hat came up to me. "You've been here for a while. Where are your parents?"

The mention of them started the tears again. They turned on each time I thought about them. He rambled a lot more questions in my direction but I said nothing. I made a promise to Mother that I would not tattle. Soon more grown-ups showed up, including the police who asked a lot of the same questions like where my parents were or if I had run away from home. I said nothing.

The police officers escorted me to the station. My backpack contained my parents' identification, provided by Farrah. That started a search for my family, which took two days before they located my aunt, Vera. Meanwhile, they gave me food and a bed, but I couldn't eat or sleep. Anytime I closed my eyes, I saw Pig Lady cutting off my sister's head.

My aunt arrived, embraced me, and took me to her home. It was odd to be there without anyone else. Because she lived so far away, I didn't know her. During the initial week, Vera persistently pressed me for information about what occurred and the whereabouts of her brother and sister-in-law. I remained silent. I hadn't uttered a word since Farrah left me in Tulsa. How could a child possibly articulate witnessing a woman resembling Farrah Fawcett decapitating people and consuming their body parts? So, I kept quiet. The only sounds that came out of my mouth were those when I woke up screaming in the dead of night, reliving those horrific events repeatedly in my dreams.

After an exhausted search, the police and detectives stamped the case as unsolved and stopped looking. Even if I could speak or wanted to speak at that time, I would not have been able to tell them much. Then, I didn't know where it had happened. I didn't know where I was at the time. And I honestly didn't even know what city it was that Farrah dropped me off in. They figured out it was Tulsa based on where the police found me and the bus ticket. Something catastrophic had occurred, and Vera accepted their deaths and acknowledged that must have witnessed it all.

She eventually sent me to a doctor, hoping to pry open the psychological torture chamber that was my mind. The doctors concluded my muteness was post traumatic stress and would be only temporary. Even though I wouldn't speak, I continued to function like any normal kid. I had an incredible amount of energy, which I spent on running around the yard in circles. My appetite was a bottomless pit. I ate all the time. Oddly enough, it balanced out perfectly; despite the excessive intake, I never gained weight. Compared to kids my age and height, I was the epitome of the perfect girl in terms of exercise and body weight.

Medical doctors confirmed there was nothing physically wrong with me. Psychiatrists assured Vera I would eventually speak again, someday. At that point, Vera stopped pouring money out for the same results. I was 10 years old and hadn't uttered a word in two years, except for the screams that woke me up every night.

My silence persisted until I turned 13. Vera had become accustomed to my nightly terrors, always there to comfort me back to sleep. But when it happened in broad daylight, Vera's protective instincts brought her rushing into the bathroom. There, she found me on the toilet, clutching a piece of toilet paper stained in blood.

"Oh, Cora. You're not dying. This just means you are no longer a girl. You've become a woman."

The words, long buried under the muck and mud of 1977, surged out of me like a wild, untamed river. "No! No! No! They will kill me. They will eat me. No! I can't be a woman. Stop it! Please, stop it! Put it back!"

I had always been afraid that those women, or others would come for me, but at 13, I became a woman, and I was positive that Pig Lady would come for me because I was old enough for them. They'd sink their teeth into that part of my body and rip me to shreds. It flung me into a fit of terror because I was now ripe, and Vera confirmed it. The killers in the diner didn't want me back then because I was a girl, not a woman.

It was a short-lived period, lasting only a day. Yet, within that time, I lost so much blood that I fainted, prompting Vera to rush me to the hospital. It felt like someone had pulled the plug, draining me of every ounce. I stayed in the hospital for three days while doctors ran tests, ultimately concluding that it was a fluke and I was back to normal, minus an iron deficiency.

Over the next few years, my life revolved around a series of mental and physical doctor visits. Physically, each time I menstruated, I passed out due to blood loss. Fortunately, my periods lasted only a day. I went through test after test. Medical professionals prescribed birth control to manage or reduce the blood loss during menstruation. It worked until they attributed my gradual weight loss to the medication. This led to monthly hospital visits again because, without the drug, I bled profusely for an entire day.

On top of this, regardless of how much food I consumed, I kept losing weight. It wasn't sudden, and neither I nor Vera, who saw me every day, noticed it. It was when I returned to school after a summer break that a teacher noticed my weight loss and suspected it might be an eating disorder. I was 15 years old and weighed just over 100 pounds. The average weight for someone my age was about a 128 pounds, although most of my peers in school weighed more than that.

The doctors attributed it to the irregularity of my periods, but that teacher convinced Vera that I must be bulimic. Vera knew I ate all the time, and in her eyes, if I ate, it meant I must have been vomiting it back up when no one was looking. Despite my repeated verbal protests—yes, I spoke all the time by then—no one believed me.

Initially, I spent a month in a rehabilitation hospital where they closely monitored my food intake and observed me around the clock, including my bathroom routines. As I mentioned, the weight loss wasn't drastic. When the psychologists confirmed I wasn't vomiting my food and that I maintained the same weight for an entire month, they released me.

During that two-year period, from when I became a woman until the accusations of bulimia arose, I saw a psychotherapist. This was to unlock the suppressed memories of what happened to me as a child, especially after finding my voice again and the flood of words poured out. *They would kill me and eat me.*

The therapists relentlessly pressed me with questions about who "they" were, but all I could respond was, "I don't remember."

That wasn't the total truth. I remembered who *they* were. Pig Lady and Farrah. Of course, I remembered *them*. The deaths were vivid pictures in my mind. I could describe my sister's open eyes staring back at me, her head detached from her body as some other woman stuffed her face between the legs of the headless torso. Or how Farrah sucked the nipples of my mother's breasts into her mouth like they were spaghetti noodles. Yes, I remembered it all like it was yesterday; however, I didn't want to talk about it.

During that period from seven years old until…, I formed a highly unhealthy infatuation with Farrah Fawcett. Every time I went to the store and saw something about her, my fingers got sticky like glue. I tore pages from magazines and slipped them into my pockets. Trinkets from classmates found their way into my backpack. I even stole items if they had something Farrah related like articles from magazines, stickers, and dolls. I amassed a shoebox full of these collected things under my bed. For Christmas and birthdays, Vera allowed me to choose something from the Sears catalog as my present, and without fail, it was always something Farrah related.

Did you know there was a mannequin Farrah head and you could style her hair? A glamor kit so little girls could become hairdressers. Vera bought one of those for me. Before I grasped the concepts of birds and bees, straight, gay, or anything sexual, I used to take the Farrah head and roll it on the ground toward me, much like my sister's head did. I'd sit for hours on the ground looking at her and even painted the base of the neck red.

After becoming a woman—and after I realized no one came to kill me—my use for Farrah's head changed. On that one day a month, before it got too late in the day, I placed the doll's head between my legs and rubbed myself against it until my body shook, making a bloody mess of Farrah's face. Then I would take her into the shower with me and clean her up, just to repeat a month later.

You might cringe reading this, but there's nothing wrong with adolescent masturbation. Studies show that by the age of 14, a significant 62 percent of male teens and 46 percent of female teens have engaged in it. Parents often share stories about teen boys and their discoveries of adult magazines hidden under beds, but rarely discuss their daughters' experiences. Society treats female masturbation as a taboo topic. While boys might engage in it more frequently, girls also take part. Personally, I was someone who did it once a month, though I didn't realize it was masturbation back then.

Brunswick Stew

During the years before I became a "woman," I consumed a lot of food. I mentioned earlier that any time we went out to a restaurant, I always ordered some sort of stew. They had pot roasts, beef stews, and this thing called Brunswick stew.

I hadn't learned about Beef Bourguignon when I was scouring the menus, so this name stuck with me for a while. There needed to be some sort of stew recipe other than the infamous Beef Bourguignon. It's an easy way to mask the flavor of human meat in a stew for those people who haven't grown accustomed to this odd texture, and it has become my specialty.

Brunswick stew is something every great Southern cook knows how to make. It's a thick, tomato-based stew made with barbecue sauce and a mixture of leftover smoked and roasted meats like pork, chicken, and beef.

It typically includes corn, lima beans, or butter beans, and a few simple spices to give it just a touch of heat. There's some debate about its origin, whether it comes from Brunswick City, Georgia, or Brunswick County, Virginia. Either way, its original recipe included squirrel meat, rabbit meat, and other wild game. Because of this, it allows us to use all our excess parts, such as livers, kidneys, and intestines, along with some good ol' meat.

This stew bursts with bold flavors, combining a Tex-Mex vibe with Southern charm. What I love most is its balance of protein and veggies—a wholesome meal for the family. Plus, the best part? It freezes perfectly. Whip up a large batch, enjoy your servings, then portion the rest into quart-size freezer bags. Lay them flat in the freezer for easy storage and simply thaw in the refrigerator overnight when ready to eat.

INGREDIENTS

1 1/2 tablespoons canola oil

1 large onion finely chopped

2 cloves garlic minced

2 1/4 cups chicken-style broth (PAGE: 23)

2 tablespoons tomato paste

1 can (14.5 ounce) fire roasted diced tomatoes

1 1/2 cups frozen corn

1 1/2 cups frozen lima beans

3/4 cup barbecue sauce plus more for drizzling

2 tablespoons brown sugar

1 tablespoon Worcestershire sauce

1 1/2 teaspoons hot sauce

1/4 teaspoon fresh ground black pepper

1/8 teaspoon crushed red pepper

1–2 pinches of cayenne pepper

4 cups of whatever protein you have available

INSTRUCTIONS

- Heat oil over medium heat in a Dutch oven or heavy stock pot.

- Add the onion and cook until tender; five-six minutes. Reduce heat and add the minced garlic cooking for one minute while stirring constantly.

- In a small bowl, stir the tomato paste with 1/4 cup of the broth and then pour it into the pot.

- Add the remaining broth, diced tomatoes, frozen corn, lima beans, barbecue sauce, brown sugar, Worcestershire sauce, hot sauce, ground black pepper, crushed red pepper, and cayenne pepper to the pot over medium-high heat. Bring to a low boil.

- Reduce heat and simmer for 15 minutes.

- Add the meaty proteins and let it simmer for about five more minutes. If desired, season the stew with salt and more pepper to taste.

- Spoon into bowls and drizzle with more barbecue sauce.

NOTES

This is my ultimate recipe for repurposing leftover meats and bits that may not take the spotlight. It's a versatile dish that can use a variety of meats—great for innards or cuts not typically featured, like steaks. Perfect for cleaning out the fridge. You can toss in extras like potatoes, butter beans, celery, or okra. When guests come by, I enjoy pairing it with coleslaw, cornbread, and applesauce.

Chapter 4

At 16, I'd just begun my junior year of high school. Still reserved, friendless, and looking like a bag of bones. In contrast to the chubby girls with baby fat, the boys found my figure striking—nice firm breasts and a skinny waist. The notion of being a lesbian wasn't even on my radar; the word and its meaning hadn't reached me or anyone in my school. 'Gay' was the term in use, often used to describe effeminate boys.

Perhaps if I were to be analyzed now, people might assume my obsession with Farrah was sexual. I didn't think of her that way, or at least not yet. At this point in my life, I was only reenacting what I had seen: Farrah's face between my sister's legs. And while having the doll rubbing against my lady bits felt good, I had been so closed off from most everything in the world that I didn't understand that this was sex. I didn't truly understand why I did that. Maybe it was to prepare myself from the inevitable, to be killed by sadistic people.

Every night, I still woke up from nightmares of being killed by her and her companions. Vera had long stopped checking on me during the night, becoming tired of the same thing all the time. It's kind of like crying wolf, how many times does one keep showing up when there was not much more they could do? Therapy proved useless, and I eventually stopped attending sessions. It seemed like everyone had lost hope in me, completely giving up.

I found myself alone a lot. Vera had met a man at work, and he occupied most of her energy. Since she wasn't wasting it on me, she used it on herself. I don't blame her. She didn't sign up to be a mother figure, it just happened. Vera was young, vibrant, and attempted to be as motherly as she could to me, though she had her own needs too.

A week before the Sadie Hawkins dance, Tyson Evans sidled up to my locker with his cunning smile and perfect teeth, asking, "Who are you asking to the dance?"

I was surprised because we had never talked. I replied, "No one."

Tyson embodied that all-American, perfect image—a football player and swimmer, adored by everyone or at least wanted by most. He was in my English class, which was how he knew me. I was mostly invisible except for the catcalls and whistles when I walked down the halls. What I saw in the mirror—pale skin, dark circles under my eyes, and dark hair—wasn't what they saw. They saw a tall, skinny goth chick who maybe did drugs and got wild in bed. My tendency to wear mostly black didn't help dispel the image.

"Give me a week. If you like me by Friday, ask me to the dance," Tyson said.[1]

In those days, social media hadn't yet invaded our lives, shielding us from the fear of having our embarrassments broadcasted. In that moment, what I felt was relief from the isolation, finally having someone unafraid of me. Being wanted felt good. High school in the eighties was either the best or the worst; there was no in-between. I'd spent the initial two years in hospitals and doctors' offices. With Vera having given up on finding a solution, I was free from appointments and could finally live a little.

"Fine!" I slammed my locker and followed him and his friends to the football field, where we missed third period and hung out under the bleachers.

By the end of the week, I invited Tyson to the Sadie Hawkins dance. He charmed me, said all the right things, and made me feel beautiful for the first time in my life. Before the dance, he picked me up in his fancy, caramel-colored Camaro with matching shirts he chose for us. We posed for photos, and he proudly paraded me around the gymnasium, proclaiming that I was smitten with him, which I wasn't. Surrounded by balloons, streamers, music, and a facsimile of love, I found my sense of belonging and normalcy. The haunting thoughts of bodies being dragged across linoleum floors faded into the background. I became lost in high school life.

Throughout that entire night, we danced only once. For the rest of the evening, he stood in a group of his football peers, and I found myself cast off with their dates. They were discussing an upcoming party at Tyson's house, and when they asked if I planned on going, I responded, "I guess, if Tyson wants me there."

At the end of the night, he asked if I wanted to join him and his friends back at his place. With Vera all but moved out of the house and living with her new boyfriend at his apartment, there wasn't anyone at my house waiting for me. I agreed and let him drive me to his place where everyone was partnered up and making out on various sofas and chairs. Typical high school movie scene, right?

My social skills sorely lacked, and so did my making-out skills. No one had ever kissed me in my life, but the dimly lit living room felt sexually charged with the hormones of teenagers. Ones who had much more experience than me. My nerves were on edge, causing my body to tremble; my brittle bones clattered underneath my skin. We were in the kitchen when he offered me a beer to calm my nervous system from overheating.

His hand gripped mine, then he tugged it, ordering me to follow him upstairs to his bedroom. Behind the closed door, he took off his shirt and pressed his body against mine, snaking his hand up my shirt where he cupped my breast. There wasn't anything graceful about his grip; much like he was grabbing the football to prevent it from dropping from his hand. Still, I shook. Every inch of my body ached from being overly taxed by stress. With no experience in this, I let him guide me backward, where he hooked the edge of my pants and pulled them over my hips, taking my underwear with them.

His body pushed me down, so I was on my back looking at the ceiling as he kissed his way down my body. When he reached my stomach, I tensed. He kept going, his hands spreading my knees apart. Again, I tensed further, but that didn't stop him from nestling his face between my legs. As soon as his mouth reached my nether region, I screamed.

It was as if a pail of blood rained upon me, flooding me with the reality of my nightmares coming to life. Tyson was one of them. He wanted to kill me, to tear the flesh from my body, starting between my legs. I kicked him, knocking the ball of my foot into his nose and breaking it. Blood gushed everywhere as he screamed along with me. I rushed to grab my clothes, fearing for my life. There wasn't even enough time to get them on before his friends burst through the door. I was naked and living my sister's horror, where I believed all of them were ready to overtake me. I tore from Tyson's home and hid behind a bush until I had my clothes back on.

Abby, a girl from inside who had been dating a defensive linebacker, stepped from the house and called my name. "Cora, hello? Are you still out here? Are you okay?"

I didn't answer. The adrenaline coursed through my veins, blood pumping so fast I became lightheaded. Tears streamed down my face, and I just wanted to go home, where it was safe. Go back to a time when I wasn't a woman, and no one wanted me. Through the bushes, I watched as someone else came out of the house.

Robert, a second-start quarterback, joined Abby. "I should get in my car and try to find her. She shouldn't be walking the streets if she's scared or hurt."

"I'll go with you," Abby said. As they trekked down the lawn, they must have heard my whimpers because they peered into the bushes and Abby said, "Cora, is that you?"

Still believing everyone wanted to kill me, I took off running. Barefoot and all. Robert, being the fast football player he was, took after me and caught up with me. When his arm grasped mine, I screamed again. Lights on every property illuminated, and many residents stepped onto their porches.

"Stop. I'm not going to hurt you. Please," Robert said, trying to soothe me like Vera once did.

When Abby caught up with us, she wrapped her arms around me, encircling me with her warmth and trying to calm my blubbering. "You're fine. Are you okay? Hurt? Tell us what happened."

What was I supposed to say to them, really? I wasn't hurt. I was scared because I thought Tyson wanted to kill me but there was a sliver of doubt in my mind, maybe he wasn't a human-eating murderer. The longer I stood there and reasoned reality and the psycho-trauma of my past, I summed up the entire ordeal as a bit of a mind flip. "I'm fine. Panic attack is all. I just want to go home."

Robert and Abby offered to drive me back to my house. The entire trip, I sat in silence while they grilled me about Tyson, insisting that he had done something to me that I refused to admit. I only shook my head.

They dropped me off, offering to stay with me, but I declined any more of their hospitality. The house was a haven, as no one had entered it to take my life. As soon as I was alone and in the sanctuary of my domain, I broke down. On my knees in the middle of the living room, a deluge of tears drained from my eyes. I couldn't help but realize that what Farrah, Pig Lady, and the others had taken from me was much more than my family. Those people in that diner robbed me of my childhood, my innocence, and the social development of a youth. I trusted no one. There were no friends. And what remained with me was a recurring nightmare that prevented me from experiencing the wonder of adolescence.

What I remember next is waking up on the floor of my living room when Abby showed up the next morning. During all the chaos from the night before, I forgot to lock the front door—something that wasn't much of a habit in eighties suburbia. She arrived to check on me, which was the start of a wonderful friendship.

After cleaning myself up, we went to school together. Immediately, I was the talk of the day. Gossip of my dramatic role as the crazy, unhinged Sissy Spacek had traveled overnight, and I suffered even more post-traumatic stress disorder from that. As if I already didn't have enough on my plate. Abby did her best to shield me from it, even if she had no clue why I had reacted how I did.

Tyson showed up with a bruised face, very much pissed off that I benched him from playing in an important game. When he showed up at my locker, threatening to get back at me for what I had done to him, Robert stepped in. "Back off, alright. You've done enough damage to her."

There were two sides to the Tyson/Cora debacle. Those who believed Tyson about how I turned into Carrie White, and those who believed Tyson was a predator, who lost to someone defending herself. I was neither of those things. Still, Robert became my bodyguard and protector. Abby became my best friend. And we formed an alliance.

Abby had been dating Tyson's best friend, but when the school became divided, she broke it off with Kevin Jenkins. In suburban St. Louis, relationships become all too incestuous. Robert and Abby had been friends since elementary school. After believing their friendship was more than that, they hooked up with a very clumsy and awkward loss of virginity. Afterward, they vowed never to do it again and remained close friends. Tyson had attempted to persuade Abby's younger sister into a quickie in the past, which was most likely the reason Abby assumed Tyson wasn't innocent in my case. After all the rumors Tyson spread in my direction, I never corrected anyone who thought he had attacked me that night.

During the snowy Christmas break, Abby introduced me to William Daley and his friends, a bunch of stoners who smoked a bowl before class every morning. This was the first and only time I smoked pot, not liking how it made me feel. While I didn't judge them on their usage, I just didn't partake. The great thing about this group of friends was their lack of judgment or criticism. Abby and William began dating, and when Robert returned from his vacation, he asked me to be his girlfriend—a vast difference from Tyson's remark on how he conned me into our one and only date.

Robert Barker was a nice guy, maybe too nice for his own good. He never pressured me into doing more than hanging out and kissing. On Valentine's Day, we went out on a romantic date to an Italian restaurant where I ordered a spezzatino, which is just a fancy word for Italian beef stew. See. There are some things that didn't change. It was gross, but I didn't complain.

When he returned me to the house, I invited him inside since Vera had all but moved out by then. Groceries magically appeared on the kitchen table once a week, with some cash for incidentals. It wasn't long before we snuggled on the couch with our tongues wrestling. Groping never bothered me, so Robert snaked his hand up my shirt. Unlike Tyson, Robert was slow and gentle. We had yet to seal the deal; I was still a virgin. When I didn't stop his mouth from finding my breasts, he took that as a sign for more, which I allowed him. Much like Tyson did, he kissed down my body and undressed me. His lips traveled up my legs and when his head got too close, I jerked upward and told him to stop.

I expected anger to come out, especially after overhearing comments about girls being teases and leaving guys blue-balled. He took my protests as stopping completely, and he flopped next to me with his erection at attention.

"I'm sorry. That wasn't what I meant," I said as I took his hand. "Just don't put your head there. We can still have sex."

"Are you sure? I don't want to pressure you if you're not ready," Robert said, being a gentleman and all.

"I'm sure." With that, I adjusted myself on the sofa, leaning back so he could climb on top of me. The act itself was very barbaric, something I didn't enjoy, but it seemed to be what teenagers did—or at least everyone I knew. I squeezed my eyes closed because I didn't want to understand why he grunted like he did. The less I saw, the better. I had already seen enough horror in my life, and his animal sounds led me to believe this rabid wolf-like form tore away from his human flesh, shedding layer after layer of his man form and transforming into a hairy, anthropomorphic hybrid while on top of me.

When I squinted through the lids of my eyes, trying to tell myself it was some imaginary fantasy, I saw his snout extending from his gaping mouth with bloody fangs dripping red saliva. I told myself not to scream; so again, I pressed my eyes closed and allowed this feral creature to couple with me like a ritualistic rite of passage.

As his body relaxed, I opened my eyes again. Robert had returned to his mortal, human state, no longer possessed by the demon spawn of Satan. My breath exhaled and my body relaxed, as I had survived. He kissed me, very loving and caring as he always did, but he noticed my disconnect.

"Was it that bad?" he asked.

I didn't know what to say. How could I tell him it felt like he had stabbed me with a sword and punctured my heart in the process? "No. It was just my first time, and I wasn't sure what it was going to feel like. You were great. I'm sure next time will be better."

Oh God. Next time? Did I really tell him there would be a next time?

He only stayed for a few minutes more, long enough for us to dress, then he stated he loved me and casually bid farewell until the next day at school.

Alone, I stepped into the bathroom, wanting to wash his disgusting stench from me. I peed first and noticed a crimson stain on the paper. At first, I believed it was the start of my day of hell; therefore, I entered my bedroom, grabbed Farrah's head, and placed it between my legs. I don't think I had ever pushed it into me as hard as I did that day. My body pulsated around her head so much that I clenched my thighs together. If she had been human, I might have killed her.

Ultimately, I fell asleep with Farrah's doll head between my legs. When I woke up in the middle of the night, she wasn't there, but I found her next to me. Without cleaning her, I did it again and when I finished, I set her head on my dresser. The next morning, I woke to find Farrah's smiling face caked with dried red smears, coating her like paint. She never again joined me in the shower because I grew fond of her face, looking as if she had eaten strawberry ice cream.

---

1. No, the movie *Can't Buy Me Love* had not come out yet.

Spezzatino

For this recipe, I'm jumping ahead in the timeline of my story. After becoming an official chef, my employer sent me to various countries to develop my craft, one of which was Italy. Wow, it was an amazing trip. My employer, who you will meet later on in the story, had determined there was a very underground society growing for folks like us—those fond of human flesh. This, of course, was before the internet and dark web where you can easily locate like-minded individuals who share your indulgences.

On this trip to Italy, I worked with a renowned chef who catered to the wealthy, women who paid very well for a delicious meal of a succulent breast, or the juicy cunt of some peasant woman. Yes, that is very much a rich delicacy.

During these two weeks of intense cookery lessons, I tasted some of the finest cuts of meats, sampled some savory meals, and learned that not only do good things come to those who wait, but it is so very worth it—such as a Prosciutto di Parma, for which the sweet and delicate body of a woman goes through a long preparation marked by rigorous and perfectly cadenced processing phases. The seasoning alone can last up to three years, during which the scents and fragrances of the Parma hills cure a woman's body to create a product of excellence. Can you imagine holding a cut of meat for three years before sinking your teeth into it?

Some of us don't have the luxury of that type of prolonged discretion, and we have to process and consume our meat sources as quickly as possible. That's why I chose items that are easy to cook but also tasted amazing. The beef spezzatino is one of the most traditional dishes in Italy, widely enjoyed throughout the country. In northern Italy, it's commonly eaten with polenta, while in the southern regions, it's usually served with just a few thick slices of crusty bread.

This dish is so common that there are endless variations, and every family has its own recipe. Spezzatino is quite similar to many other beef stews from around the globe, especially the Hungarian Goulash and the French Beef Bourguignon. The key difference with spezzatino is the use of extra virgin olive oil instead of butter for the soffritto and the nice aftertaste given by the Italian herbs.

Now, I'll emphasize that for this dish, you must use extra virgin olive oil. As much as I advocate for natural oils, using a virginal woman or man does not replicate the quality. Just because someone hasn't fucked yet, doesn't make their oils and fats "extra virgin."

INGREDIENTS

1 small white onion

1 small carrot

1/2 celery stalk

3 teaspoon extra virgin olive oil

1 pound meat (preferably off the back), cut into 1-inch cubes

1/8 cup all-purpose flour

1/4 cup white wine

2 cups meat stock (PAGE: 23)

1 sprig rosemary

2 sage leaves

1 bay leaf

1/2 teaspoon black peppercorns, partially crushed

Salt, to taste

2 medium potatoes, around 10 ounces total

INSTRUCTIONS

- Clean the onion, carrot, and celery for the soffritto and chop them finely.

- Add the vegetables into a heavy bottom-deep skillet along with the extra virgin olive oil. Turn on the heat to medium and sauté for five minutes, until the onions turn translucent.

- In the meantime, pat the beef cubes dry with a paper towel and coat them with flour. *Remember, no one likes wet meat.

- When the vegetables are ready, add the meat to the pan. Stir for a couple of minutes to sear the beef on all sides.

- Deglaze with wine. When the wine is completely absorbed, cover the meat with stock and add the rest of the ingredients except the potatoes.

- Cover with a lid and turn the heat to low. Then, let simmer for two hours, stirring occasionally. If the stew becomes too dry, add a ladle full of water.

- After two hours, cut the potatoes into 1-inch cubes and add them to the stew. Cook for another 40 minutes, stirring as little as possible.

The stew is ready when the meat becomes very tender, and you can almost tear it apart with a fork. The sauce should be quite thick. Turn off the heat and serve with polenta or with some wonderful bread. Because this makes a healthy helping, it's a sumptuous meal to serve to friends. If you are looking to turn someone so you don't have the desire to eat them anymore, this is a great starter meal.

Chapter 5

For William's birthday, his parents bought him a cream-colored Chevy G20 Beachcomber van with brown pinstripes. He removed the mid-seats in the rear so he could have his own little love den on wheels. When spring break hit, he wanted to take it on the road with Abby, who wanted me to tag along. Of course, I didn't want to be a third wheel, so I convinced Robert to come with us.

The four of us drove southwest from St. Louis to Springfield. The open highway and deserted cities along the way flashed memories of my past. I had given little thought to the drive or where my nightmare happened; it was just a continuous loop of memories with no real details about where it had taken place. Another flood of memories returned when I saw signs for Tulsa, Oklahoma, when we got into Springfield since it was the next major city. Route 66. Hell Kitchen. Maybe we could see it from the road.

"We have an entire week. Why don't we keep going on Route 66 until Wednesday, see how far we can go, and then return home," I said, volunteering an idea that I'm sure no one had thought about.

Everyone shrugged, and William continued on. We stopped off and on, filling up with gas, grabbing snacks, and taking bathroom breaks on the side of the road when needed. Going in the opposite direction, the sights did not look familiar to me when we passed through the stretch of land between Tulsa and Oklahoma City. Again, 10 years had gone by, and I wasn't at all sure this was where it happened. I saw nothing.

At the end of the journey west, we spent the night camping in Albuquerque, New Mexico. When the sun came up the next morning, I stepped from the van and took a moment to myself. I pondered whether all of this had actually happened. As much as I lived through, part of me questioned my sanity or if I was bat-shit crazy and needed to be in a mental ward. I saw things that weren't there. Robert continued to change into a werewolf each time we had sex. I glanced over my shoulder constantly, fearing the Pig Lady might be nearby. My weight had dropped under the 100-pound mark, which both Abby and Robert voiced concerns over despite my gorging on rancid-tasting hamburgers. There was even a moment when I believed someone had drugged me, which I mentioned in a doctor's visit. That came back negative. So did every other test except for that pesky iron deficiency.

With no medical reason for my issues, I had to concede that my problems were psychosomatic, especially when the cacti in the middle of the desert turned into green prickly creatures, coming to life and chasing me back into the van. When my paranoia woke up my sleeping friends, I confessed to them I was off my rocker because of an incident that took place on June 29, 1977.

"What happened on that day?" Abby asked, wrinkling her brow as she did.

I didn't want my friends to know. As much as I wanted to be normal, I feared I never would be. "That's the day my family went missing," was all I said.

"Dude. Like taken in a UFO? Aliens?" William asked, after taking a hit of some little pill.

I laughed it off. "Maybe."

William offered me one of his little pills, insisting I should clear my mind. Abby took a different approach, stating I needed to cleanse my aura, throw everything away, and move out of Vera's house to start over. There was a part of me that thought all my issues would blow away with the wind once I said them out loud.

Instead, I just laughed, said nothing more about my trauma, and convinced Abby and William to leave so Robert and I could be intimate. It had been a while since we'd done anything. And each time it happened, I went into it hopeful that I was cured. Each time, I thought if he didn't transform into a snarling, rabies-infected dog-wolf, I would finally be free of the illness. While I still didn't let him go down on me, I did open myself to him, but nothing changed. His mutated form tore through my body, ripped me apart like a wishbone. I cringed and held my breath until he went soft.

I didn't blame him but he stopped in the middle of it, not finishing and not saying much to me. I felt bad. I'm sure he felt worse. Nothing like having a girlfriend who looked as if she was disgusted by the entire act that was supposed to be loving and fun. We didn't speak again as we started our quiet journey back to St. Louis.

Once past Oklahoma City, my eyes remained focused on the road ahead, scanning for any signs of familiar landmarks. Somewhere around the midpoint, William pulled off the highway to fill up. We tumbled out of the van and into the service station, which had a little grocery store attached to it. My eyes caught sight of a familiar mustard-colored mid-size station wagon off to the side. A flash of lightning struck my mind like it hit an electric pole, and sparks blew out of my ears. A mental deluge of rain poured through my veins, flooding my soul with memories of racing from this vehicle into a diner whose sign read "Hell Kitchen." I almost froze. It was my father's station wagon.

With Abby leading the way, her hand clasped tightly in mine, we entered the store. She found the bathroom as I wandered, my eyes darting in every direction, looking for a lady with a turned-up snout like a pig. Instead, my eyes fell upon a girl around my age with wavy brown curls. We locked our gazes, both of us dropping our jaws in a momentary stop of time. It was as if some electrical current had chased from my brain to my groin, but at that moment, I had never wanted Farrah's head more. I could have ridden her for hours.

Abby's presence shook me out of this paralyzed trance, and we switched places as I entered the bathroom. Just as I was about to close the door, the girl pushed it open. We locked eyes again.

She hesitated. "You're alive."

I said nothing, still wondering if this was a hallucination of some twisted memory. Instead, I nodded and tried not to scream by suppressing the bile rising in my throat.

"Or should I say, barely alive," she said, then asked, "have you eaten?"

Again, I said nothing.

"God, I never thought I'd ever see you again."

Still nothing. I couldn't even open my mouth; it was as if someone had taken a needle and threaded it closed. Maybe she sensed my confusion, fear, or just the oblivion plane I rested upon. Her nose wiggled, as if sniffing the air. She walked to the trash can, dug through it, pulled something out, and stuffed it in my pocket. My eyes, gripped by horror, remained fixed, unable to confirm if this was real or a figment of my imagination.

"You need to eat this," she said. "The thought will gross you out, but once you do it, you'll be fine for a while. Trust me, it will taste good."

Just as she turned to exit the room, I blurted out, "Sadie!" She glanced over her shoulder. "Are you for real? Or am I just imagining you?"

"I'm very much real."

Her words propelled me forward. I lunged at her with such unbridled passion, tossing my arms around her and pressing my lips to hers. It was as if I had no self-control. During the time I should have been pining over boys, as society stated, I never did. Tyson was the all-American pretty boy who did nothing for my libido. Robert, as sweet as he was, never excited me either. This girl in front of me

MASTERING THE ART OF FEMALE COOKERY

seemed to bring out a different side of me. Every part of my body tingled with excitement, including the part where I liked to place Farrah's doll head.

Inside that bathroom, at that moment, I knew no restraint. I pawed her body like a kneading cat, suckling what I could of hers. She did the same, shredding my clothes off and tossing them to the side while she glided down my body with her tongue. Just as her mouth touched the patch of fur between my legs, I trembled. She was one of them. Once a girl, now a woman. Sadie was the person they sent to find me and eat me. This is what I had prepared myself for and the moment had come. Instead of fighting against it, I succumbed to my fate. "If you're going to kill me, do it."

If Sadie were to kill me, I'd let her take my life just as my mother and sister had lost theirs. I had all but given up on life at that moment. My body dropped with my back against the wall, knees bent, and legs spread. Sadie's head nestled between them, much like Farrah's head did, but this time, she did the work, and I relished my impending doom.

When it was over, I walked out of the restroom with new realizations. One, oral sex didn't kill me and I actually liked it. Two, she gave me a life-saving gift, which was in my pocket, wrapped in toilet paper. And three, someone might have just cured me[1].

---

1. Only the first of these three was correct. Oral sex will not kill you. But her gift was not a lifesaver—more like a temporary bandage. And there is no cure. It's feast, or famine.

Cowboy Burgers

Hamburgers are one of those accessible ways to satisfy that meaty craving. There is always some ground meat in the refrigerator. So when time is limited, I recommend a hamburger.

You might think that having a boring burger all the time will get old. If this is where you are on your cannibal journey, which there is nothing wrong with, I'm going to provide you with a little recipe to spice up the boring burger. If you don't have experience in curing your own ham and bacon (PAGE 19), you can purchase a pack of bacon from the store. As long as you are consuming mostly human proteins, you are good with a few shortcuts.

For me, I always divide my meat into one-pound portions and keep it in the freezer until needed. Depending on how many burgers you are making, you can double this recipe if needed.

INGREDIENTS
1 pound ground beef

4 slices bacon, cooked and crumbled

2 small jalapenos, chopped

1/2 cup shredded cheddar cheese

1/4 teaspoon salt

1/8 teaspoon pepper

INSTRUCTIONS

- Mix all ingredients together and make patties. For one pound of meat, you can make two or three patties.

- Grill for about 15 minutes each side, depending on your preference. I prefer a medium-well burger. That is an internal temperature of 150 degrees.

Notes: The great thing about being a cannibal is that you do not have to worry about salmonella or e-coli. If you want to eat it raw, be my guest. There is just something about the dripping fats and oils that come with cooking meat that makes a burger delicious.

Chapter 6

Now my story comes to my senior year in high school. Robert and I were still together, as were Abby and William. Over the past year, I had learned the secret to taming the growing hallucinations in my head, which calmed many of the explosive panic attacks. That was human blood, though at the time, I only believed it was menstrual blood. Like an elimination diet in reverse, the only thing different in my life was what Sadie had given me and suddenly the mind trips ceased, as did the night terrors. Because of this, it mended the relationship with Robert because I no longer saw the wolfman coming at me with his giant appendage. I could get through sex without gluing my eyes closed with a petrified, scrunched face. Even though I had relaxed, I had not felt the same emotional charge that I did when Sadie had made me feel better than Farrah's head ever did.

I still had this insatiable craving that continued to grow more needy. At least once a day, I found myself in the bathroom at school, sniffing and rummaging through the garbage for leftover remnants of students' times of the month. I equated my disease with vampirism, which it wasn't; but what does a 17-year-old know? It was the only thing that made sense. Blood came into my mouth and seemed to calm me, much like William when he took a little white pill. Those weren't my finest moments, but it worked, so I went with it for the time being. There were a few other things it did to me, as well. My own menstrual cycle leveled out while I was hornier than most of the teenage boys in my high school.

Just before the Christmas break, during one of Robert's football games, he suffered a severe injury. So much so that they called the game, and medics carried him off the field. Abby and I followed them to the hospital, where the doctor confirmed he completely tore his anterior cruciate ligament, which is his ACL. This would require surgery to fix, ruining his chances for a college scholarship.

Neither of his parents were optimistic about his chances, which destroyed Robert's happiness and mood, turning our merriness into a gloomy winter. His lack of celebration caused me to spend less time with him and more time with Abby and William.

On New Year's Eve, St. Louis became a hot topic on the news when police located the bodies of several female campers in Horseshoe Lake State Park. The grisly murders left these women with their throats sliced, their legs severed at the knees, and their genitals ripped from their bodies. During that time, the police had no suspects.

About a week later, the news outlets stated police found a female college student, much like the campers: throat sliced, legs cut off, and the flesh of her womanly parts removed. When another round of victims suffered the same ill fate, the police issued an official warning for a serial killer targeting women in the area, suggesting we travel in packs and never after dark.

Abby said I should stay at her house with her parents since I lived alone in Vera's small brick bungalow. I took her advice, packed a few bags, and headed to her place for a bit.

One afternoon, we had planned to meet William after school at the deli across from the campus. Since he had already graduated the year before, he wasn't with us as much. When we crossed into the lot, I noticed the mustard-colored station wagon parked. My eyes darted around, and my heart pumped blood at a furious pace, almost stinging my veins as my body temperature rose. I knew that was my father's car. It was the same car at the gas station. If two and two equaled Sadie, I didn't want to get into William's van when it pulled up for us.

"Come on!" Abby said as she entered.

I mumbled my hesitation. "Uh. I. You go on without me. I'll meet you at home."

"Are you sure?"

When my tone reassured her, accompanied by a plastered smile, she closed the door and went on her way. If this truly was Sadie in the parking lot, I reasoned, she could be at several stores. Instead of hunting her down, I waited by the car and let her come to me.

It took about 10 minutes for her to exit the supermarket. She strolled up next to me, leaning her back against the car to match my stance. "You are a hard one to find."

"So, why were you looking for me?" I asked.

Sadie pushed away from the car, stepped in front of me, and placed her lips on mine. There was something so feral in how she took me, not caring if anyone saw. Her hand slipped down my pants as she nuzzled into my neck. The hazard was, I cared. I popped the handle of the car, opened the passenger's back door, then pushed her inside. Within seconds, we were both rubbing each other raw until our breaths fogged up the windows, and our animalistic grunts caused our mouths to unlock.

After we had appeased our desires, we sat up straight in the backseat and savored the lingering taste of satisfaction. Sadie leaned over the front bench, pulled a crumpled-up newspaper from a bag, and unwrapped it. On her lap sat a half-eaten drumstick. It might have been grayish in color but with the shape and skin on it, there was no mistake it was of the human kind. Her teeth sank into it, tearing meat and skin away from the bone. My eyes widened in terror as I remembered the graphic news reports detailing the mutilation of females and their missing limbs.

She offered me a bite, almost as innocent as one would offer a French fry. When I declined, she asked, "Haven't you eaten yet?"

My mouth refused to open, even with the saliva pooling up from my taste buds. I shook my head.

"Cora!" Sadie sat up. "That's your problem."

Finally, my mouth opened, defending myself. "I don't have a problem."

She tore another piece of meat away with her teeth, pulled it from her mouth, and shoved it into mine. I spat it out, but she caught it and, despite my protests, she shoved it in again and kept her hand over my mouth. "Eat. Chew it and swallow it."

I mumbled, shaking my head. But as the drool covered the meat, my tongue bathed it, savoring it like a melting piece of chocolate. Finally, it gravitated to my molars, and I bit down like it was a tender piece of steak. That's when she removed her hand. I moaned my pleasure as if this was the greatest thing I had ever tasted. My head drew back as I swallowed, basking in its wonder. I pulled the uncooked turkey-like leg from her hand and cannibalized it without coming up for air.

During this time, Sadie told me everything I needed to know about this life. As a child, Sadie's clan fed me something that contaminated my body. It stayed dormant until my body expunged its first womanly cycle, which unleashed a deadly virus that had been eating me from the inside. In order to stop it from killing me, I have to feed it what it wants. Human meat, untainted by that very contaminate. Eating Sadie would do nothing for me; it would be as pointless as biting into a flavorless piece of cardboard. I needed to find someone who had not yet transformed. My mind went directly to Michael Jackson's "Thriller" video, and how I was now a zombie, not a vampire. Yet, I wasn't dead or undead.

"How do you know who's infected and who is not?" I asked with a piece of calf meat in my mouth.

"Smells are the easiest way. Are your senses heightened when you're around someone who is bleeding? Are you drooling? Are you horny as fuck?"

"Yes. All the time." This was true. That's why I couldn't find anything at school to quench my insatiable libido. I felt like a teenage boy wanting to dry hump anything I touched.

"Then they are ripe. If you can't smell them..." Sadie shrugged her shoulders and left the sentence hanging there in the air.

"So only women?" I asked, curling up my nose at the thought of all of it, though I couldn't stop chomping on the drumstick in my hand, gnawing to get every scrap from the bone.

"No. Only women can get infected, but all men are fair game to eat It's just there is something about fresh blood seeping out of a person that turns us into wild animals. If you wanna go after a guy, go right ahead but they're much stronger and they'll probably harm you before you can kill them."

Sadie pulled the hunk of flesh from my hand, taking a bite for herself. The severed limb reminded me of the women killed in town. "Did you kill the campers and the college girl?"

She smiled, grinning from ear to ear and holding up the leg. "Of course; I needed to eat. And so did you, I see."

The 10-year-old memory returned, vivid as always, where I watched Pig Lady and Farrah, and their team of human-eating monsters, devour my mother and sister. It made sense. They were not just attacking them like wolves protecting their domain. They were feasting on their uncontaminated bodies because both of them were women—not children—and they had been menstruating. I remembered how Farrah's nose had twitched in the mirror, smelling their bleeding bodies. And Sadie, outside the diner, told me they wouldn't kill a child. I wasn't ripe yet.

"I won't kill someone. I'd rather die," I said.

"Suit yourself, but since you have just dined on this delicious redhead, your pain will start all over again. You'll go crazy. The pain of your body eating itself from the inside. I'd just hate to see you suffer like that."

I glanced at Sadie next to me. Her wavy curls were messy on top of her head. Her clothes were dirty, but I hadn't felt that attracted to someone besides my unrequited crush on Farrah Fawcett. There was something that still made little sense to me. Slowly, my words came out. "If I'm only excited by uncontaminated blood, why do I want you so much?"

She pressed her lips together, hiding her smile. "That's a totally different reason."

With that, she tossed the newspaper and leftover meat stick in the front seat and climbed on top of me.

Roasted Legs

The most common and likely pieces of meat to cook, and the easiest, are drumsticks. If you want to engage in some caveman kink, cook these on a spit rod over an open flame. Maybe even have a little Lūʻau with your friends and roast a couple of legs while you are at it. But, if you are looking for a simple way to make great-tasting drumsticks that an entire cannibal family can carve into, this recipe is perfect for a nice Sunday meal in the oven.

Ingredients
Avocado oil spray
1 human calf drumstick (bone-in, skin-on, cut at ankle & knee)
1 cup butter melted

Seasoning Mix
1 tablespoon sea salt
1/4 tablespoon black pepper

1 tablespoon garlic powder

1 tablespoon dried thyme

1 tablespoon paprika

Instructions

- Preheat the oven to 450 degrees. Fit a rimmed roasting pan with a rack and spray the rack with avocado oil.

- Mix all the seasoning ingredients in a bowl and combine thoroughly.

- To prep the meat, lather with soap and shave off any excess hair. Pat the leg dry with paper towels. Brush it all over with melted butter and rub it with the seasoning mix.

- Place it on the roasting rack and lightly spray with avocado oil.

- Roast, uncovered, for 30 minutes, until the skin is browned.

- Loosely cover the leg with foil to avoid scorching the top and continue roasting it until the juices run clear when pierced with a fork and an instant-read thermometer not touching the bone registers 165 degrees, about 30 more minutes.

- Remove the leg from the oven and allow it to rest, still covered in foil, for 10 minutes before serving. *Do not skip this step.* It will enable the internal temperature to climb a bit more and the juices to redistribute and settle.

Chapter 7

It was the weekend of the annual Fourth of July festival, when the city set up a carnival inside the fairgrounds. Abby and I, along with Robert, had graduated. This was the era in which our parents (or more so my friends') afforded us the liberty to expand our horizons, or at least that was only half of the intended plan. Because of Robert's injury, he did not get offers to play college football. This meant he and I were staying in St. Louis after high school. Before his accident, I imagined I would follow him to wherever he landed, start college there, and we'd be married. That didn't happen.

By then, I had learned I was a human-eating cannibal and that the only person I wanted to touch sexually was Sadie. Because of Robert's lack of a football scholarship, he could get a job on his own, go to college on loans, or work for his father at the hardware store his family owned. He had gotten a job at the fairgrounds for the festival, despite our protests that he spend the holiday with Abby and me, then confirmed he would start learning the family business.

Abby took the summer to do what she wanted and would be off to college in Springfield in August. Vera had put the house on the market, so I would soon need to decide my future because I'd be homeless as soon as either Abby went to college or the house sold. William was William, slumming in his parents' basement where he smoked pot most of the day. His family was a lot like he was: hippies who still lived in the past. I was 99 percent positive I could have camped out at his place, and they would be none the wiser.

Then there was Sadie, a welcome breath of fresh air amidst Robert's pity party and my carnal desires. While I should have been at Robert's side, nursing him back to health, I was with Sadie, learning that I enjoyed the softer touch of a woman. God, I look back on her now and can still picture her perfect breasts, firm ass, wavy curls that tickled my nipples when she came on top of me, and those lips. What I'd give to taste her again, but alas, that cannot happen.

As Sadie became a permanent fixture at the time, I passed her off as a daughter of an uncle by marriage from Oklahoma. My friends didn't mind having another person tagging along. She stayed with me at Vera's most of the time, until the house sold, and provided me with the food we needed to survive. I didn't ask where the pieces of meat came from, and she didn't tell me. It was the perfect solution to the problem. Despite always feeling the urge to ravage her, I resisted and kept our make-out sessions private for as long as we could. That was until one day I really needed a sexual release while at William's place. A slip of not locking a door, and William found me on the bathroom counter at his place, with Sadie's head between my legs.

My eyes widened, and Sadie stopped mid-lick as the bathroom door opened. I had a feeling he'd tell Robert because of some bro code.

"I won't tell if I can watch," William said as he closed the door with him inside.

Sadie shrugged, dropping her head back down to my clit and bathing me with her saliva. He did nothing but watch, yet I hadn't come so hard as I did at that moment. I don't know what caused it. William did not turn me on at all. He did nothing for me. But Sadie. Oh, Sadie. I believe that the idea of no longer hiding allowed my mind and body to open so wide it triggered whatever was holding me back.

After I had come, William left the bathroom and walked into the living room where Abby had been smoking weed and watching some game show on the television. He dropped his shorts, then removed hers, and they began fucking like rabbits. I think it shocked Abby to find us in the middle of the living room with them, at first. But we didn't stare. Instead, Sadie sat next to them on the sofa, and I kneeled before her and indulged in my favorite sweet treat. Her.

At first, Abby questioned my sexuality, which I defended myself by saying I was in love with Robert but liked how Sadie felt. It wasn't a bold-faced lie. I had been in love with Robert, or at least thought I was, but that dwindled the longer Sadie was by my side. Plus, Robert's increasing negativity, most likely due to his lack of college prospects because of his injury, had caused him to distance himself from us more often than not. Sadie, on the other hand, was eager to go along with William's increased sexual exhibitionism tendencies.

I knew I'd never have that sexual freedom with Robert. The one time the four of us—William, Abby, Robert, and I—spent a cozy evening together, Robert got angry when Abby took William to her mouth and sucked him off. I attempted to soothe the mood by doing the same, but Robert pushed me off him and walked out of the room. So much for free love. Sadie, however, let me be as free as I wanted.

After the fireworks spectacle, we bolted out of town and camped in William's van just outside of Mark Twain National Forest. Robert didn't come, so the four of us parked and enjoyed the clear sky filled with some of the brightest stars I had ever witnessed. When the morning sun rose over the dewy landscape, I woke to find Sadie not beside me. William and Abby were inside the van, curled up under blankets, but I was alone.

Quietly, as not to wake my friends, I called out for Sadie. There was no response. I ventured for a while, searching for her, when I stumbled upon a lone tent under a hickory tree. My stomach growled in the morning air as the scent of a fresh body wafted up my nostrils, igniting a vigorous sniffle like a bloodhound on the move. The closer I came to the tent, the stronger the odor. With each step, the temperature of my body rose, scorching my skin until I wanted to rip it from my bones. My sex was a boiling pressure cooker, whistling its signal to nature that it needed to be released. And when I pulled back the tent's opening, I saw Sadie gorging on the neck of a dead man.

She looked up at me, pieces of skin and hunks of flesh dangling from her mouth. Her face was smeared with a crimson glaze, glistening in the morning's light. Since learning of my condition, Sadie had only provided me with leftovers, packed up in a newspaper and already dried from the drained blood. Never had I seen the aftermath of her killings. Much like the merciless slaying of Marie and Mother, there was an abundance of blood pouring and draining from her victim's neck, coalescing under his head and back. The sensations lit me up like a Christmas tree, and I was a mere child, begging for permission to dive into my gifts.

When Sadie rose, sliding back to give me access, I dove into him with an insatiable greed. My eagerness caused Sadie to laugh as she joined me, sinking her mouth into his cheek and tearing it away from his face. And when both of our stomachs were full, we took care of the other primal need to sustain us until next time. Afterward, we strolled to the little stream closest to the tent, cleaned our faces and hands, then returned to the van. Outside it, William was emptying himself by a tree.

"Ran off for a morning quickie, I see," William joked as he shook his stick and tucked it back in his pants. Within a few moments, we were back in the van and on the road again.

When we reached the outskirts of Tulsa, Sadie and I felt a growing arousal because of a lingering fragrance enveloping us. Much like in the woods when the camper's blood loss had led me to him in a hypnotic trance, this aroma tugged at our senses and drew our attention forward. There was only one reason for this. Abby. She was the oven, baking a delightful cherry pie between her legs.

Being trapped in the van with her was torture, intoxicating. Normally, we could walk away to calm the hidden beast. But being so close was like asking a parched mouth not to crave water. When Sadie and I realized what had caused the mouthwatering sensation, there was a glint in her eye that said she craved the kill. I shook my head in protest. That was out of the question.

Over the past year, I made it a point to distance Sadie from Abby whenever this monthly moment happened upon us. While I had the moral compass that led me to choose my own death over another person's, Sadie had grown up in a world where death and human consumption were part of everyday life. While she searched for prime opportunities like a sleeping camper, Sadie had no reservations about killing someone for an afternoon snack. They were nothing more than a bag of Doritos to tear open and pop in her mouth.

The longer we remained in the car, the more that determined stare radiated from Sadie and pinned on Abby. Nothing I did to distract her worked, because I knew that murderous look. I understood the primal beast that lurked just under the surface. I recognized her cat-like twitch, ready to pounce on its prey.

"William, can you pull over? Please. Now!" I hollered as soon as Sadie's foot pivoted for traction.

There it was. My worst nightmare came true. Sadie lunged forward with her hand reaching for the knife she always kept in her pocket. I screamed as William swerved. My grasp tried to tug Sadie back, but she was faster than me, slicing Abby's neck in the blink of an eye. Blood sprayed the windows as the van veered into the dirt, smacking shrubs as it came to a screeching halt. Sadie swung her arm in the air, attempting to take William out, but he elbowed her in the face, knocking her back.

From the glove box, William pulled a gun, pointed it at Sadie, and without hesitation, pulled the trigger. Two bullets entered her chest, sending her flying back and hitting the rear doors. The knife flew out of her hand, which I picked up. In my anger, I raced toward William and stabbed him in the gut. In and out. Multiple times. As much as I hated Sadie for killing Abby, I hated William more for shooting Sadie.

As William slumped forward, the gun in his hand fired once more. This time, striking me in the thigh. I tumbled backward. The sheer pain of the wound made a belly full of nausea rise up, but I swallowed it down as I closed my eyes. The pinch of my eyelids caused a waterfall of tears to stream down my cheeks.

Was this truly my life? Three dead bodies on the side of Route 66 in the middle of nowhere, Oklahoma? I'm not sure how much time I spent mourning the situation, but just as I succumbed to the fact that I needed to move both William and Abby to the back of the van and drive it home, the side door opened.

I was startled, thinking it was the police, and I'd have to explain why there were fresh dead bodies piled up. Instead, it was as if Heaven's gates swung open, and a radiant woman emerged, illuminated by the glowing sunlight. One with sandy blonde hair that feathered back on the sides. Were angels actually singing in my head? Because in that moment, my eyes saw my savior. Farrah.

I blinked repeatedly, trying to focus on the woman who said, "Holy shit!"

She glanced to the side and muttered another set of profanities. She hoisted herself into the van and closed the door. Hurriedly, she pushed past me and pulled William and Abby toward the rear, almost tossing them on top of Sadie, then started the van, which skidded into gear. It lurched forward, kicking up dust behind us. I tried to lift myself up to see where we were going, but my leg wouldn't allow it.

The woman glanced over her shoulder at me. "Just stay down."

I did just that, leaning back on William's leg, and closed my eyes. The van swerved, hit a bump, then bounced as she drove us off somewhere. As the van slowed, I heard the crackle of dirt and gravel underneath the tires. We were off the road, maybe even off the grid, when it stopped. I opened my eyes to confirm it was none other than the woman from the diner looking back at me, her eyes filled with pity. I'd have given myself that same look, much like Vera's when nothing she did fixed the constant disappointment that is my life.

Farrah said nothing, only shook her head, then pushed up from the driver's seat toward the back and rushed to Sadie to check for a pulse. Her eyes pinched shut and head dropped. "Fuck," she mumbled, then check the others.

Abby was dead with her throat cut open. As soon as she turned William over and saw the mangled meat that was his stomach, we both knew he was dead. She glanced at me. "Are you okay?"

At the same time, we glanced down at my leg. After climbing out of the van, Farrah, who still looked as I remembered her, only older, placed her hands under my arms and pulled me from the vehicle. My leg was a bloody mess. A burgundy wetness soaked and stained my pants, pinning them to my leg. When I tried to put pressure on the wound, a searing pain radiated through me, spasming my nerves. It felt as if my bone splintered and tore open my flesh as I howled in agony.

She didn't bother to close the van door, leaving the massacre inside visible as she hurried me to a small wooden-framed home where she placed me on a table, propping my leg up on the top of a chair. My head dropped back onto the wooded slab, which I felt was my deathbed, while she fumbled with my pants. It must have been the loss of blood that had caused the strange ideas to cross my mind, but at that moment my only thought was about her head, her mouth, and I instinctively spread my legs wanting her to comfort me like her mannequin facsimile had in the past.

That wasn't where she went. She gave me a pair of socks and then said, "Bite down, this is going to be brutal."

With the socks placed in my mouth, my muffled screams came as she dug into my thigh with needle-nose pliers and extracted the bullet lodged into the flesh. Vomit pooled in my mouth but I couldn't swallow it. It came out like a gusher when I turned my head. Alcohol covered the gaping hole, streaming down my leg and puddling below me like I had pissed myself. More muffled screams. She cleaned it up the best she could, then stabbed a needle and thread in me, over and over, tugging the flesh back together, then tying the thread tight to keep my blood from oozing out like the chocolate from a molten lava cake. Somewhere in the middle of it, I drifted out of consciousness.

Deep Dish Cherry Pie

When I have a lot of time on my hands, I find one of my favorite things to create is a casserole, or in this case, meat pies. When dicing up the meat for this recipe, I recommend a nice, lean cut from along the back—probably just under the shoulder bone, down to about the waistline. Along this portion, most people have a leaner section. If you stay more toward the center, keeping away from the sides, this is ideal. Those stupid love handles have a lot of fat on them.

Because this is going into a pie crust, aim for your diced pieces to be about half an inch big. If you cut them much bigger than that, it will take longer to cook and your bites will be too chunky. Ideally, try to keep all the ingredients around the same size. Concerning the port, I recommend a tawny port, which is aged in wood and takes on a brownish color, as well as more complex flavors of toffee, chocolate, and caramel.

Ingredients

For the meaty pie filling

21 ounces dark meat steak, diced

2 carrots

2 celery sticks

2 parsnips

8.8 ounces chestnut mushrooms

2 red onions

14 ounces cherries

6.75 ounces tawny port

2.1 pints beef stock (1 liter)

1 bunch of thyme

1 bunch of parsley

2 cinnamon sticks

1 pint beef stock (page: 23)

salt and pepper

For the pastry

8.8 ounces plain flour

4.4 ounces salted butter, cubed

pinch of salt

1 beaten egg

Instructions

- First off, prep all the vegetables and fruit. Half and pit the cherries, and peel and chop the vegetables to the recommended size.

- Tie the thyme and parsley together with some kitchen string (so it's easy to fish out at the end).

- Take a large casserole pot and heat a small amount of oil on a medium-high heat. Season the diced back steak well with salt and pepper and add to the pan to sear. This will take around five minutes. You are looking to get a nice solid gray color all over the pieces of meat. If you brown it, the meat will lose flavor in the pan and not in your pie. When done, remove the meat cubes (leaving any juices in the pan) and put to one side.

- Put the cherries into the pan and add the port. Once the mixture comes to a boil, allow it to simmer until it has reduced by half, which usually takes about 10 to 15 minutes.

- Add in all the vegetables, the herbs, cinnamon sticks and one liter of dark meat stock. Bring to a boil, then reduce the heat to a simmer and pop the lid on. Leave to simmer for 90 minutes.

- After 90 minutes, add the cooked meat and the rest of the meat stock. Pop the lid back on and cook for a further 90 minutes.

- While you are waiting for the venison pie filling, you can make the pastry. Put all the ingredients into a large bowl and rub the butter into the flour using your hands until it resembles fine breadcrumbs.

- Add a couple of tablespoons of water and mix in so that it forms a dough. You may need to add slightly more water if it's not held together. Wrap the dough in plastic wrap and put in the fridge until ready to use.

- Once the pie filling is ready (it should still be moist, but not have a lot of runny liquid), take it off the heat and fish out the herbs and cinnamon sticks.

- Take the pastry out of the refrigerator, divide into two equal parts and press each of them out (using a sprinkle of plain flour to stop it sticking) until it is the thickness of a nickel.

- Press one into the pie pan, up the sides of the dish. Spoon the mixture into a pie dish, on top of the pastry.

- Brush a little beaten egg around the edges of the pie dish and gently lay the second pastry over the top. Press the edges down and trim anything hanging over the edges.

- Pierce the pastry several times with a fork or a knife. Sprinkle generous pinches of salt and pepper on top. Brush the pastry with the beaten egg and put in the fridge for half an hour.

- Preheat the oven to 400 degrees.

- When ready, take the pie out of the fridge, brush again with beaten egg and then put in the oven for around 40 minutes until the pastry is a golden brown.

Chapter 8

When I woke up, I had forgotten where I was and panicked as my eyes landed on an unfamiliar setting. My body shot upward from the sofa, rising to my feet, only for the pain to pull me back down. I needed to assess my condition before dragging myself up and, painfully, managing a few steps.

This wasn't the same house I had been in 10 years ago. The room was a hodgepodge of furnishings, ranging from mid-century to discounted bargain bin items. It was dirty, most likely from the dusty landscape outside that found its way onto the floor from shoes coming inside. I glanced out of the house's window and saw dusk settling around the bare trees. The van was no longer in front of the home, not that William or Abby could have driven it away, unless that morning had been a dream.

It was not. I glanced down at my body to see a thin coating of dried blood on my leg and a once-white, now-soaked bandage over what I knew were my Frankenstein stitches. As the burnt orange sun dropped behind the trunk of a tree, the room dimmed even more. With no pants on, I shivered, and goosebumps pricked my skin like a fluted pastry wheel rounding my legs. Just then, I heard a door close at the back of the single-story home, causing me to jump.

Almost as if it was improper to be wandering about, I hurriedly tried to return to the sofa before being caught. All that did was turn my legs into pudding, and I stumbled forward.

From the doorway, the woman chuckled. Then she walked forward and aided me to my feet. "Let's get you back to the couch."

I mumbled a "Thanks" as I plopped down, then asked, "Where's the van? And my..." The words didn't come out, as I didn't know what to call the pile of carcasses I left in the back seat.

She exhaled and sat down next to me. "It's around back."

I think we both skirted the actual issue, which I saw as a dilemma. My eyes cast a long gaze at her, studying the features that were still beautiful. There seemed to be a mutual longing, though she broke eye contact like we were in a staring contest and she blinked first.

She pulled herself up from the sofa. "I should make some supper."

The clanking of pots and pans sounded a little heavier than they should when cooking—more like slamming them around. Once again, I felt more like a burden than a welcomed visitor. Ready to ask for the keys to William's van and leave, I rose from the sofa once more. By the time I hobbled my way to the kitchen, the banging of metal had ceased, and Farrah had her head buried in the palms of her hands.

I didn't know why I felt so compelled to care for her, but I opened the refrigerator, drawers, and cabinets to pick out ingredients and began sautéing up some meat—probably human—and veggies. There weren't many seasonings, not like Vera had in her kitchen, so it was pretty bland with what I had to work with. It also would have been much better over a bed of jasmine rice, though I couldn't be picky at that moment—also, I hadn't learned to be picky yet.

Her words were barely audible as she pulled some plates from the cabinet. "Thank you."

The crickets' song crept into the silence through the opened back door as we sat with the plates in front of us at the little two-top table on flimsy chairs that shook at the joints with any movement. As soon as she brought the fork to her mouth and the food reached her palate, she moaned in appreciation.

One side of my mouth curled. "It could have been better with more preparation."

"It's perfect," she said, still sulky, with the whites of her eyes tinged a shade of pink. She rubbed them in between bites.

As much as I wanted to ask for reassurance, I left the conversation about Sadie alone until she brought it up. There were a million more questions I had, including ones about my family and my morbid curiosity about what happened to their bodies. All of which I hated to ask, but there was an enormous elephant in the room. This woman had killed my parents 10 years ago, and we were now face to face, sharing a meal like friends, not addressing any of it.

As she finished the last bite on her plate, there was a hesitancy within her. Unsaid words lingered around us as she shook her head in apparent wonder. Then she pushed away from the table, tossed her plate in the sink, and stepped out the back door. Much like her, when I finished, I paused, pondering my immediate future and questioning what was next before I cleaned up the mess in the kitchen. Alone inside the house, I wandered at a slow pace—still in pain from the bullet wound—and explored each of the rooms in this little two-bedroom home. One room still contained toys, much like Sadie's room when she was young. There was a bathroom next to it. Not even thinking to ask for permission, I entered as my bladder called, rushing into the room as soon as I saw it. As I sat down, the moment seemed surreal. All I could do was shake my head at myself in the mirror.

When I came out, I continued exploring. There was another, larger bedroom—a double bed, one dresser, and a nightstand containing a lamp with a dingy white shade. The sheet and blanket were a tangled mess on top of the mattress.

Before entering, I glanced over my shoulder to see if I was still alone. From the open window, I heard Farrah outside. Without turning on the light, I entered and allowed the hallway light to guide me as I opened her dresser. Not that I was hunting for anything in particular, just trying to sense who this woman was other than a murderer. Inside, I found clothes, a few magazines, books, a Bible, and trinkets. I touched nothing.

In the small nightstand next to the bed, I did the same. I opened the drawer and found loose keys, coins, paper money, a vibrator, a gun, and some bottles of medicine. Of course, I picked up the bottles, which all had different names on them, both men and women. Her victims, possibly.

The window to the outside was above her bed, and I peered out. In the darkness, I saw her figure digging into the dry dirt next to a barn-like structure. After watching her for a moment or two, I left the bedroom and joined her in the yard.

As soon as she saw me, she stopped digging. "Go back inside, please."

I didn't listen. Instead, I moved closer to her. That's when I noticed a lump of a body covered with a blanket. I asked, "Sadie?"

Her head dropped, chin to her chest. "Yes. Now go back inside, please."

The unmistakable flutter of her words told me she had been crying. While I couldn't make out the dampness on her cheeks, I felt it in the surrounding air, coming from her heart. Still, I didn't obey her wishes. "Was she your daughter?"

The shovel's tip plunged into the ground, perhaps harder than necessary, as she forced it in and continued her grave digging. "Not biologically, but yes. I guess you can say that."

After the summer with Sadie and learning about what I had become, I didn't fear this woman who had taken my family from me. It was more of a sadness—for her, for me, for Sadie. We lived with this need to feed on a substance that required others to die. Kill to live. Because of this, we were murderers, which ultimately put a target on our own backs. One mistake. One wrong move, and we'd be the ones dead, like Sadie. As I watched this woman place Sadie's body into the ground and cover her with dirt, I wondered what had happened to the others. William and Abby's bodies were what Sadie had wanted. They were a viable meat source, uncontaminated by the disease.

"I'm sorry about Sadie," I said, unsure of what other words might help ease her loss.

"Hazards." That one word summed it up.

There were hazards and dangers to this. My father could have found his way into the diner and killed her and Pig Lady as they tore into the warm flesh of Mother and Marie. Another camper could have heard the moans of Sadie and me when we devoured a sleeping innocent man. Just as William always had his gun, Sadie had always been in danger of being shot–long before this tragedy.

When she finished the job, she ducked into the barn. As the door opened, I peeked inside from where I leaned against the post. Unable to see anything, I pushed off and followed her, limping with each step. As I reached the door, she slipped around it, almost startled to see me there.

"You should rest," she said.

"Where are my..." Still, I couldn't say the words.

"I took care of them while you were asleep."

"What does that mean?" I asked. And there it was. I needed her to say it. I needed the verification that she was, in fact, a cannibal and she ate them just like she had eaten my sister.

We were close. Very close. So close that I could see the layer of dust coating her skin. When she licked her lips, they turned a rosy shade of pink against the gray of her dirty face, much like a corpse wearing lipstick. It took all my willpower to resist the desire to kiss her, to erase her pain with mine. Despite the lack of glimmer in her sunken eyes, she had been the woman who invaded my dreams every night. Dreams that used to be filled with horror and death, but now I yearned uncontrollably to feel her head between my legs, consuming my orgasms like a milkshake being slurped through a straw.

As her hands clutched my biceps, I could feel the heat radiating from her palms. She had the same intense look in her eye as Sadie did just before going down on me. I thought she'd do it but suddenly, she pivoted, redirecting our path away from the barn, her touch guiding me with a gentle push. "Again, you need to stay off your feet and rest."

She closed the barn and escorted me back inside. By this time, it was the middle of the night. I still had no clue how I'd move forward in life, or how to explain to William's and Abby's parents that they were dead—and likely consumed by both Farrah and myself.

Inside the house, she led me to the sofa where she inspected the wound, medicated it, and reapplied the bandage. My leg draped over hers, her hand resting on it. Her finger inched upward. Her eyes darted to mine. As they did, her body tensed, and she said, "By morning, you should be well enough to get back on your way."

There was a poignant silence between us. Ten years ago, she hadn't wanted me to leave her, or Sadie. She had asked me to stay with them. Now, like a dismissive mother hen, she was pushing me out of her nest to fend for myself in this cruel world.

"Get some sleep." With a gentle motion, she disentangled herself from beneath me and repositioned my legs, propping them up on the sofa. Afterwards, she covered me with a cozy blanket, making sure I was snug and secure for the night.

Baked Breasts

At 18 years old, my mind often raced with thoughts more fitting for a teenage boy, particularly about all the amazing things I wanted to do to this woman—my very own Farrah Fawcett wannabe.

She had the perfect body, at least to me. And I couldn't stop imagining her with no clothes on because that is what teenage minds do. Right? At that age, everything is new to us. Sex. Naked bodies. After Sadie introduced me to the wonders of the female body, I looked at everyone in some sort of sexual manner. I wondered if their breasts would fit in my hand. I wondered if they had big areolas or small ones. If their pubic hair was curly or straight. I don't think there was a person whose body I wasn't curious about. With Farrah, I wanted to know it all... down to the taste of all the parts of her genetic make-up.

But at that moment, while she nursed me back to health, my eyes remained fixed on the shape of her breasts. That's why I decided to share a simple recipe for handling the tender breast meat. This dish will not work with a male specimen, so for this meal, you will need to toss aside your feminist morals and eat a woman. You don't have to be a lesbian, but if you are, you will enjoy this a little more.

INGREDIENTS

4 skinless plump breasts, pounded to an even thickness

1 tablespoon melted butter or olive oil

1 teaspoon kosher salt

1/2 teaspoon freshly ground black pepper

1/2 teaspoon garlic powder

1/2 teaspoon smoked paprika

INSTRUCTIONS

- Cut the breast away from the body, as close to the torso as possible. If you enjoy suckling a human breast, this is a good time to run your tongue over the tender breast. If you cut away while the woman is alive, there are nerve endings still active that will pucker the nipples under your mouth. It is truly fascinating. So, suck them until they soften. At that point, you can bite it and rip it away from the breast meat. You need the hunks of flesh to be skinless.

- Pound out the breasts. Take out some of that anger. We all have it, because we don't want to be cannibals. I'm sure you agree; this isn't fun. Use a meat tenderizer on the flat side, just like bludgeoning someone with a hammer.

- Brine the breasts. Fill a large bowl with one quart of warm water and 1/4 cup kosher salt. Stir the mixture until the salt dissolves.

- Add the breasts and let them sit in the mixture to brine for 15 minutes, or you can also cover the bowl and refrigerate for up to six hours.

- Remove the breasts from the brine, rinse them with cold water, then pat them dry with paper towels.

- Heat the oven. Preheat to 450 degrees.

- Season the breasts. Place the chicken breasts in a single layer in a large baking dish. Brush both sides evenly with the melted butter or olive oil.

- In a separate small bowl, whisk the salt, pepper, garlic powder, and paprika until combined. Sprinkle the seasoning mixture evenly over the breasts on both sides.

- Bake until the chicken is no longer pink, about 15-18 minutes. You should use a cooking thermometer to determine exact doneness, as it will depend on the thickness of the chicken breasts. The thickest part of the breast should read 165 degrees.

- After cooking the breasts, remove the pan from the oven, transfer the meat to a clean plate, and loosely tent the plate with aluminum foil. Let the meat rest for at least five to 10 minutes.

- Eat and enjoy!

Notes

For a crispier and slightly browned top on the dish, consider turning the broiler on high during the final three to five minutes of cooking. Broil the meat until it's cooked through and has a golden finish. Keep a close eye on it to prevent overcooking or burning.

Chapter 9

When morning arrived, the sun peeked through the window, casting peculiar shadow patterns onto the floor from the wind-blown lacy drapes. It felt like being on a psychedelic acid trip, watching the patterns evolve into a kaleidoscope of colors and shapes. I stirred before pulling myself from under the covers and quietly limped down the hall. Peering around the half-closed door, I found the woman, whose name I still didn't know, asleep.

After emptying my bladder and glancing at my still-bare legs, I shuffled to the kitchen. Inside the cabinets were the usual items—coffee, bread, and such. Like at home, I brewed a pot of coffee while standing in front of the open refrigerator, contemplating what to eat. That posed a bigger issue. Though there were a few eggs, butter, milk, and some veggies, most of what filled the refrigerator were bags of meat. The freezer was no different. Variety clearly wasn't on this woman's list of priorities. Just like

Sadie, she was probably content with gnawing on a human leg like a dog chewing a rawhide.

In the pantry, I discovered an old can of peas that I mashed up with butter, milk, salt, and pepper to create a gravy. While going through the bags, I found a piece of flesh that I half-heartedly carved into a deli number seven. Using some flour, I battered it and cooked it up into a makeshift chicken-fried something-or-other.

I might have roused her once breakfast was ready, but it turned out to be unnecessary; she halted in the doorway and leaned on the frame. "I thought you'd be gone by the time I woke up."

Shaking my head, I replied, "And go where?"

"Home. Anywhere. Away."

A snicker escaped through the air from my nostrils. "Yeah, well. I don't have a family or a home. And unless I'm walking, I don't really have a way to go anywhere."

With the pea puree simmering, I plated the fried meat and used the same oil, just drained, to fry up an egg for the top. Perhaps a bit much for breakfast, but I didn't know what else to do. I was in a strange predicament. The unspoken truth weighed heavily, especially when I brought up my absence of family. Why? Because she killed them. She knew that. And so did I.

With a pour of coffee, she sat down at the little table and gazed out through the early morning dew that had settled on the windowpane. When I set the plate in front of her, her attention turned back to me.

Not moving from her side, I towered over her. "Do I get to know your name?"

She stared at me for what seemed like an eternity before she said, "Dianne."

It wasn't as exotic as Farrah, but my disappointment was only temporary as I sulked to my chair across from her. Again, we ate in silence. She wasn't much of a talker. I watched her tear into the meal as if she hadn't eaten in weeks. The more I ate, the more I put this mysterious meat in my mouth, the more I wondered if I was eating my best friend. While it tasted heavenly, I wanted to vomit. It was easier when Sadie provided me with a no-named piece of meat. There wasn't a face attached to it.

I finally said it: "Where are my friends?"

Her voice was still low as she answered, "I've taken care of them."

That wasn't the response I wanted. For the first time, I raised my voice, rising to my feet as I slammed my hands on the table "I know you're a fucking cannibal. Now tell me where they are!"

Again, there was a long pause as I stood across from her, my hands pressed into the wobbly table. Saying nothing, she scooted from the table and walked out the back door. I followed her as she led me to the barn. In the corner was a deep freezer. With a key, she unlocked it and opened the lid to reveal their bodies cut and quartered, wrapped in plastic and stuffed within this square icebox. Abby's face stared back at me as her head sat on top of a stack of limbs.

My head dropped as she closed it and locked it back up. "You should leave." She handed me William's van keys from the wall of the barn and walked away.

Alone in the barn, I stood in the middle of it with my stomach twisting into knots. Not only had I gone off on this woman, Dianne, but I had forgotten that she had lost someone who she considered her daughter. Despite being mad at her, I knew she had helped me when I needed it most. She found us on the side of the road, and pulled the van into a hiding place so no one would find me with three dead bodies. Thanks to Dianne, my leg was stitched up and no longer bleeding. Sadie was six feet underground, and she was my lifeline—my food source. Since meeting Sadie, I was no longer underweight. I no longer looked like the poster child for anorexia or bulimia. In the mirror, I finally looked like a healthy 18-year-old. Leaving Dianne wouldn't have been my wisest decision, but I did.

In the van, I tore down the long drive to the street and skidded out onto the single-lane road. It took a minute for me to understand the pedals and the steering, but ultimately, I got the hang of it. In my mind, it wasn't about getting back home. I spent a few hours driving in circles, trying to locate the diner—Hell Kitchen. After coming up empty, I recognized the driveway off the single-lane road and turned onto it. The tires crackled on the pebbled dirt path lined with trees, then they skidded to a halt when I came upon Dianne's shack of a home.

Before exiting the van, I gave one last look around me. Abby's blood, Sadie's, and William's had all but dried and stained the orange carpeting a dirty burgundy. As I got out and slammed the door, I noticed Dianne standing in the front doorframe with a shotgun in her hand. She lowered it when I came out from behind the van.

At the door, a screen separated us. Her on the inside of the house, me on the outside. "I'm sorry you lost Sadie. I lost her, too."

She pushed the screen open, allowing me to reenter the home.

"Ten years ago, you asked me to stay with you. I want to stay now," I said to her.

Her eyes widened, probably wondering why this was happening–why I wanted to stay with her. It occurred to me that maybe, just maybe, she didn't know who I was. Maybe she didn't even remember me being someone who crossed her path. Maybe I wasn't even a blip on her radar. What if I wasn't as special and important as I thought I was in her world? My throat dried up, disappointment scratching the back of it as I swallowed my breath.

With a nod, Dianne said, "You can use Sadie's room."

It was unceremonious, as she walked away from me, leaving me at the front door. She sat the shotgun next to her recliner in the living room and said, "No one should ever come down this driveway. If you hear something, grab the gun. Fire and ask questions later. This one is by the chair. There are two pistols in the drawer next to the sofa. One in the bathroom drawer. I have one in my bedroom. There's one in Sadi—your room. They are all loaded."

"I don't know how to use a gun," I said as she started down the hall.

"Aim and pull the trigger," said Dianne as she stopped in front of Sadie's former room. "I'm pretty sure the clothes in here will fit."

With that, she turned and closed herself in her bedroom. I took a deep breath. She didn't seem to approve of my wanting to stay.

There wasn't much to do in the middle of nowhere. After cleaning up, I went through Sadie's things and organized the room a bit. After that, I sat on the bench in the backyard by myself. The tree-lined property remained hidden from the road. Because of that, there was no noise other than birds and critters roaming around. When I had left the property, I hadn't seen another house or ranch for a mile or so. This was the ideal place to camp, but I realized I wouldn't last long with nothing to do. Used to enjoying the city life, there was no way I could just sit all day long in silence. There wasn't even a television in the house.

When I heard the back door open, my gaze turned toward Dianne, who stepped from the house. She nodded to me as she said, "When Sadie said she saw you at the gas station, I didn't believe her. She said you had turned. I didn't know what they fed you that night. She said you were close to death when she saw you. I told her to let you go, but she was adamant about helping you. Despite my pleas, she left to find you."

"I'm glad she did," I said.

She sat next to me on the bench. "I thought about looking for you over the years, but I couldn't bring myself to do it."

"Why not?"

Her eyes directed upward as if she needed to search the heavens for the answer. "Many reasons. It just wasn't a good idea," said Dianne. There appeared to be more to the story but she changed the subject. "I had planned on making dinner, but you seem to be more creative than I am."

I laughed. "If I had more to work with..."

She interrupted me. "There's not a lot of money, but I can take you to a store if you'd like."

And that is exactly what we did.

Chicken-Fried Home Steaks

In typical teenage fashion, I'm still thinking about Farrah's breasts. Here is another recipe for use of these marvelous wonders. If a woman has larger breasts, you may need to divide them in half. We are going to use the brining recipe and instructions from the baked breasts (page: 110). Once you have skinned and brined it, we can start this recipe.

Ingredients
2 breasts, boneless and skinless (Appx 4-5 ounces each)
1 cup all-purpose flour
2 teaspoon baking powder
1 teaspoon baking soda
1 teaspoon garlic powder

1 teaspoon salt

1/4 teaspoon black pepper

2 large eggs

1/2 cup buttermilk

vegetable oil for frying

Instructions

- Add the all-purpose flour, baking soda, baking powder, garlic powder, salt, and black pepper to a shallow bowl or plate and mix well to combine.

- Add the eggs and buttermilk to another shallow bowl and whisk to combine.

- Dredge the breasts in the flour mixture, completely coating the breasts in the flour mixture.

- Dip the floured breasts in the egg wash, coating the entire breasts. Let the excess egg drip off.

- Dredge the breasts in the flour mixture a second time, getting a good coating of flour on the breasts. We want a very good and solid batter on these bad boys (girls).

- Add vegetable oil to a large skillet over medium-high heat. Heat the oil until it's 325-350 degrees. The oil should be about one inch deep.

- Cook the breasts for five to seven minutes per side until

golden brown and crispy. Or until the internal temperature is at least 165 degrees. (Repeat if necessary for additional pieces.)

- Remove the fried breasts from the oil and allow to drain on a wire rack or paper towels.

Notes

If your pan is not big enough for all the breasts, cook them in separate batches. If you have to cook in two batches, keep them warm in a 225-degree oven until ready to serve.

Chapter 10

Grocery shopping with Dianne was... how should I say? Interesting. I may have learned the fine art of restraint, growing up for five years surrounded by women who ignited a burning desire within me, yet I learned to ignore it. Conversely, Dianne required a small amount of guidance on the subject. So many times, I watched her take a deep breath and bite back what I knew as temptation. Here are the hard facts about this disease. It makes us walking time bombs of horniness, so much that the primal animals in us take over our senses of right and wrong. If one has their head on straight, they can suffer through it and deal with this urge at a later time. If not, well... You adopt the persona of a lethal predator and are highly likely to be shot and killed. Hence, Sadie's demise.

It makes sense why Dianne lived in the middle of nowhere with no one around. Without our senses in overdrive, resembling a soda can just shaken and primed to explode, we could peacefully obtain only what is essential for survival. Still, we were in the middle of a grocery store where many females were in the throes of menstruation, blood seeping from between their legs. This was heaven and hell for Dianne. I knew she wanted to sink her teeth into the warmth of their sex, drink from their pool of womanhood, then bathe her own sex with their draining blood, especially the petite Chinese woman walking toward us in the bread aisle. My understanding stemmed from the fact that I, too, yearned to unravel her like a fortune cookie and snatch away her tampon, as if my fortune lay within.

That was why consuming that camper had been so erotic with Sadie. There is something about hot, fresh blood seeping from the body that stirs the libido.

Dianne pushed the cart as I shopped for spices and seasonings. Spoiled by the filled pantry in Vera's home, I chose only the most versatile ones while giving Dianne's hand a squeeze when she needed it. We definitely could have benefitted from driving the six hours to St. Louis to raid the pantry at Vera's place. When I deposited everything I thought we could afford into the cart, we made our way to check out. At the register, she pulled William's all-too-familiar wallet from her backpack. I recognized it because there weren't many people who carried a Velcro, black-and-gray, checkerboard wallet. Whatever William had, we got. She paid for the items, then we left.

When we got to the car—a dark blue, rusted sedan with an out-of-date license plate—she let out a loud sigh. If Sadie had been with me, we would have fucked right in the middle of the parking lot. Instead, Dianne put the car in gear and settled into the trip back to her private estate, which was a two-bedroom wooden shack.

She remained silent during the entire journey back, and upon our arrival, she carried the bags into the house without uttering a single word. Closing herself in the bathroom, I could hear the shower starting. I stood by the door, listening intently. When I recognized the pants and moans of a desperate woman, I quietly opened the door and tiptoed to the shower curtain where I peeked in to see her hand eagerly bringing herself to orgasm. I don't know what compelled me to do so, but again I reached my hand inside her private space and placed my hand in hers. She gripped my little fingers, squeezing them as her body spasmed under her rapid circles.

When she came, her chin dropped to her chest as she leaned toward the wall. She didn't want me to see her shame. Our hands remained tightly interlocked as I gave her a tender squeeze. Her body was beautiful, with firm breasts and taut skin. I craved her, every inch of her. Suddenly, I missed Sadie. I missed the comfort of home, where I could confront the unfiltered desires that haunted me. With that thought, I withdrew my hand from hers and hurried out of the bathroom. If my leg had been healthy, perhaps I would've sprinted through the backyard. Instead, I headed to the kitchen and started cooking. It was my attempt to distance myself from what I truly craved… Well, we all know what that was.

For the rest of the night, I didn't see her. She didn't even come to dinner after I had prepared something delicious with what we had purchased that day. The balsamic steak sat at the table, growing cold even after I called out to her, just to be placed in the refrigerator for later. Once it got dark, there wasn't much to do in the house except read a book from the shelf. Even that didn't occupy my mind. I still wanted—and needed—the release of endorphins.

With nothing to calm the racing electrons in my brain, I crept down the hall and cautiously turned the knob, gently opening the door. It offered me a narrow view, just enough to glimpse her face beyond the door and its frame. There she was. That face. That head that I wanted between my legs. Her eyes were closed while her hand moved under the blanket around her pelvis area. That rhythmic motion told me how she felt. As my breath hitched, her eyes snapped open and her hand halted, shifting towards the door. I stood still for a moment, watching as her hand resumed its motion, all the while meeting her unwavering gaze.

When the movement became faster and her breathing deepened, with her eyes still locked onto me, I opened the door just wide enough for me to slip in. My steps were precise and deliberate as I stalked next to the bed, pulling back the sheets to find her naked body yearning to be touched by someone other than herself. Without hesitation, I joined her and nudged my body next to hers, kissing it as I journeyed downward. When I reached her sex, I removed her hand and replaced it with my mouth. As soon as I covered her, her pelvis shot upward just as her chest did, rising with the deepest breath.

The air from her lungs escaped with slight protests: "Don't. Please. I can't."

Those four words did nothing to stop me. Despite them, we both wanted this and needed this. The taste of her sent my head swimming. It was everything I had imagined it to be. The smell, the feel of her body, the sweetness. As soon as my lips pulled her clit into my mouth, a flood of warm secretions drenched my palate. More delicious than the creamiest béchamel sauce I have ever tasted. I did not stop. I couldn't. It was as if this became my gluttonous addiction; and without her, without this, I'd parish.

By morning, she was spent, yet I don't think I had once moved my lips away from her body. They remained attached to her, on some part of her body, whether suckling her breasts, kissing her arms or her stomach, or basking in her orgasms.

In all of that lovemaking I had done to her, I had not come. I glanced up from this snuggle of her body. Her eyes were closed and her breath had a slow pattern of sleep. That's when I closed my eyes, pressed my head close to her, and matched the rise and fall of her chest until I dozed off myself.

Somewhere in the middle of a dream, her body jolted upward, startling me awake. Her hurried words commanded, "Get dressed! Now!"

"What? Wh—" I stopped mid-sentence, realizing I shouldn't ask questions and should simply obey. I grabbed my clothes and threw on my shirt and shorts.

Already dressed, Dianne seized the gun from the drawer, cocked it, and slipped on a pair of shoes before rushing down the hallway. Reaching the living room, she retrieved two guns from the drawer near the sofa. She thrust one into my hand and tucked the other into her jeans. Glancing out the window, she directed, "Out the back door, don't stop. Just get in the car, passenger seat."

Unaware of what prompted this urgency or why we were moving, I complied without hesitation. I grabbed my Vans and headed to the car as instructed.

Just as I stepped from the house, I felt her hand on my back, urging me forward. "Go! Now! Run!"

In high gear, I rushed to the car, ignoring the pain searing through my injured leg. We both slammed the doors, and within seconds, we were tearing through the yard, sending grass and dirt flying behind us as Dianne hit the gas. What appeared to be a dense line of trees turned out to be more of a façade as the car plowed through the fence, and we found ourselves on a dirt road behind the property.

The blare of police sirens echoed through the yard we had just left. I craned my body to see vehicles pulling up to the house. Down another small drive, she veered off, speeding in the opposite direction. Still glancing behind me, I watched a cop car race toward where they believed we had gone, and finally, Dianne slowed, stopping next to an all too familiar station wagon. "Get out. Come on."

We jumped into that car. I didn't hesitate. Dianne edged forward, steering us south on Route 66. That was the last glimpse I had of that shabby home.

Asian Stir Fry

I hate to say this, because I don't want to appear pretentious—I am not against finding a dirty vagrant in the dead of night, but there is something to say for authentic cuisines. If given the ability to choose my human cadavers, I will plan my menus based on their ethnicities, out of respect for their cultures. Obviously, if I have a Mexican individual on my cutting board, I am automatically going to choose some Latin flavors like an adobo or a pozole.

While in Asia, I happened upon a Chinese corpse, which we used to make a spicy orange Asian stir-fry one night. We cut the skin away from their back where the meat is the leanest and took all those flavors into a wok and made a delightful meal. When I returned home, I attempted to replicate the dish using a red-blooded American caucasian. It just wasn't the same. I chalked it up to the differences between Americanized rice wines and soy sauces, but when another Chinese woman reached my butchery, I gave it another shot. I journeyed back to Shanghai through a gastronomic experience.

This is when I told myself it is all about authenticity in my recipes. If you are not fond of citrus flavors, you can leave out the orange juices.

Ingredients

For marinating the meat

12 ounces back meat strips of a native from China

2 tablespoons fresh orange juice (optional)

1 teaspoon Shaoxing rice wine

1 teaspoon light soy sauce

1 teaspoon cornstarch

For the sauce

2 tablespoons fresh orange juice (optional)

1 teaspoon light soy sauce

1 teaspoon dark soy sauce

1 teaspoon cornstarch

1/2 teaspoon sesame oil

1 pinch salt

1 pinch ground Sichuan pepper

For stir-frying

2 tablespoons cooking oil

Zest of 1/2 orange, julienned (optional)

4 fresh chilies, chopped

3 cloves garlic, minced

1 teaspoon minced ginger

Instructions

- Place "beef" strips in a bowl. Add all the ingredients for the marinade. Mix thoroughly until the beef absorbs all the liquid. Leave to combine for approximately 10 minutes. Mix all the ingredients for the sauce. Set aside.

- Heat a wok (or a deep frying pan) over a high flame, then pour in 1½ tablespoons of oil. Sear the meat until it becomes a pale gray.

- Dish out and set aside, then discard any liquid in the wok.

- Pour in the remaining 1/2 tablespoon of oil. Add orange zest, fresh chilies, ginger, and garlic. Cook until fragrant, then stir in the meat.

- Fry for one minute or so.

- Pour in the sauce (stir well beforehand).

- Plate when meat is evenly coated with the thickened sauce. Serve immediately.

Chapter 11

Returning to Albuquerque hadn't crossed my mind. I had once envisioned a future marrying Robert, somewhere distant—perhaps back east along the coast. But amid our escape, Dianne steered south and west on the highway. Throughout the journey, I didn't question our destination. So when I spotted signs for the city, I mused, "You know, I was born in Albuquerque. Wonder what happened to my old house."

We halted on the city outskirts to refuel. Digging through the glove box, Dianne unearthed some papers left by my father. They held an address from my childhood days. Grabbing a map from the gas station, we charted our way there.

Pulling up to the ranch-style home, it seemed larger than I remembered. "Are you sure this is it?"

The house numbers matched, and a car sat in the driveway, with a child on the porch playing with action figures. I opened the door, intending to approach, but Dianne attempted to halt me. "What are you doing?"

It hadn't occurred to me whether this was a good or bad idea. "I'm going to see the house?"

"You can't just walk up there and ask to snoop around!"

"I'm not snooping," I replied, stepping out of the car. Ignoring Dianne as she followed, I reached the porch. "Just chill."

After knocking on the door, a lovely woman answered. Not that I expected to see my mother's half-eaten corpse come to the door, but it surprised me to see someone else. "May I help you?"

"Hi. This may sound totally stupid, but I used to live here when I was little, before my parents passed away. I was wondering if you knew what happened to all their stuff. I guess, my stuff too."

"The Sweeneys? Wow. Uh..." she paused, then said, "I guess their lawyer would know. The house was empty when we rented it."

"So you didn't buy the house when they died? Do you know who owns the house?" I asked, still not sure why or what I wanted from this walk down memory lane.

"I guess their estate. You should probably speak with Mr. Jefferies; he's who we deal with. What's your name again, sweetie?" she asked.

"Cora Sweeney," I answered, then asked, "Do you have his phone number or address?"

"Just a second." She moved away from the door, leaving the screen open. I peeked inside as if I thought she might be lying, and I could see something familiar. When she returned, she handed me a business card. "Here's his information."

With a nod, I rejoined Dianne, and we walked back to the car. We glanced at each other, then at the card in my hand. Her eyes were riddled with questions and perplexities. I asked, "What are you thinking?"

"I'm not a lawyer, and I don't know anything about estates, but maybe you have a house here. Maybe you should go see him."

"We. We're in this together."

"You. As of right now, you've done nothing wrong or illegal. Have you?"

"Well, I'm pretty sure I've eaten my weight in human beings. I'm not quite innocent."

"But you're not the one wanted for killing…" The sentence hung in the air, as I am sure she didn't want to admit it to me.

"My family. Yes. Does anyone know that for sure? I mean, other than me?"

"Not that I know," she said with her head dropping when I had spoken it aloud.

"Fine. Then that is on your conscience, not an official wanted poster for your arrest," I said.

Yes, the nightmares were still vivid because I could still picture her munching away at their bodies. Now that I knew for sure what I had seen that day, a knot formed in my gut. Not only had I dreamed about this woman for years, but a few days ago, I had slept with her. I wanted to stay with the woman who took my family from me. She had changed the course of my life that day, and yet I seemed to be walking a tightrope, teetering between emotions. I hated her but I had wanted her for so long that I told myself I loved her. My animalistic sexual desire for Dianne was warring with my anger and grief over my family's murder.

"I've killed others, too." Her voice was a whisper when she said it, like a confession she didn't want me to hear.

I wanted to say it wasn't her fault, but I had gone five years killing no one. I had restraint; why couldn't she have had some herself? I know now, it wasn't that easy.

We ended up at the office of Joseph Jefferies, the attorney in charge of my family's estate. There was a surprised look on his face when I walked in, stinking of three-day-old funk. Remember, we tossed on dirty clothes after a night of sex when we bolted from the house in Oklahoma? We slept in the car for the past few days, and we hadn't showered since before then. We stank.

The lady in the office turned up her nose at us. "May I help you?"

I extended my hand to her with his business card in it. "I'm here to see Joseph Jefferies."

Her eyes glazed over us as if we were vagrants looking for a handout. "He's unavailable."

Behind her was a glass wall, and behind it sat a man at a desk. Most likely, that was Joseph. I glanced at Dianne, who still hovered around the door, not fully entering the office like I had. She shook her head as if I had asked her to do the unthinkable. Yes, this woman in front of us was ripe and bursting with aroma.

The saliva in my mouth had activated as I leaned forward and pressed my hands into the desk. With gritted teeth, I said, "If you don't get Mr. Jefferies now, I'll eat you alive, starting with your bleeding cunt." I couldn't believe I had just spoken my thoughts aloud; it seemed being around Dianne was weakening my resolve to act normal.

Her eyes widened at my words, and she rose from her desk as though on autopilot, moving behind the glass wall. I observed her rigid stance as she stood in front of the lawyer. She reached for the phone. When he glanced past her, he motioned for her to wait, taking the receiver from her hand and replacing it in the cradle. He approached the door, peeked out cautiously before emerging. "May I help you?"

"I'm Cora Sweeney, and I was told you represent my family's est—"

His expression softened. "Cora? Little Cora? Wow! I see it. You look just like your mother."

I nodded, momentarily forgetting the threat I had just made to his secretary. "You know who I am?"

"Of course; your father and I were the best of friends. Went to high school together. Hell, I almost dated your mother when we were—well, about your age. What, you're 17? 18? Probably 18. That's why you're here. Am I right?"

He had divulged a lot in one go, requiring me to shake off the flood of information to focus on my purpose, which wasn't entirely clear to me but was to Dianne. "Yes. Um. So, I... went by my old house, and the lady mentioned something about an estate, or something like that. I'm curious about what that means."

Glancing toward Dianne, he gave us a once-over and gestured for us to follow him. "Let's go into the office and we can chat."

As we entered the room behind him, Jefferies said to his secretary, "Joyce, this here is a client. Give us a moment."

Joyce hurriedly passed by as we entered, eager to avoid any interaction. Dianne followed suit, attempting to ward off the overwhelming desires that had gripped us both. Once the door shut behind us, there was a temporary reprieve from the odors that lingered in the room. Joseph stopped at a file cabinet, retrieved a manila folder, and positioned himself behind the desk.

Once again, he gestured for us to sit. "So, yes... I am handling the estate. Your parents had a will in place before their disappearance. When your aunt Vera conceded to their deaths about five years ago, we placed everything into a trust for you. We agreed to rent their home with the payments being directed to Vera for your care until you became of age."

"What age is that?" I asked.

"Legal age is 18." He scanned the folder and found a birth certificate for me. "And that seems to be now."

"What does that mean for her?" Dianne asked, finally speaking up.

He gave a half-hearted smile, with a questioning glare in his eyes. "I'm sorry. We haven't met; you are?"

Perhaps he felt some obligation to my well-being since he was my father's best friend, but he didn't have the right to question this woman. And what was the proper term to describe her? She was the woman I wanted to spend the rest of my life with; so girlfriend? Furthermore, I was uncertain if she felt the same way as she had not yet sampled what I had to offer.

Instead of answering his question, I just repeated what she asked, "Yeah. So, since I'm 18, what does that mean for me?"

He settled into his seat, adjusting so the chair's back faced away from us. "We'll have to draw up the paperwork to release the trust and redirect rent payments to your bank. You have a bank account?" he asked, throwing a sideways glance at Dianne.

"No. I'm... between things. Places. A gap year, after graduation, you know?"

He glanced at us once again, clearly concerned about our disheveled appearance. I understood the reason for his caution. "I'd like to get Vera on the phone with us. It's a surprise to find you in my office without so much as a phone call or conversation from your legal guardian—or rather, your former guardian, now that you are of age. You have rights to the trust, but there are legal formalities we have to go through."

At that moment, Dianne leaned closer and whispered, "Ask if you get the house if this trust thing goes through."

I took Dianne's concern and voiced it myself. "After the formalities, will my family's home become mine?"

He nodded. "Yes, although there is a rental lease on the property. Even if ownership changes, their lease is still open until..." He checked some paperwork. "Until January."

"Six months, at least," I murmured, trying to process the timeline he mentioned.

"If you're considering moving into the house, there are responsibilities you'll need to think about: mortgage, taxes, upkeep. My recommendation for you, at this age, is to allow the family to continue renting. I can help manage all of this for you, just like I am now with the trust."

I nodded.

"Let me start my paperwork on all of this. Talk with Vera. How can I get in touch with you?" he asked.

This posed a fundamental problem. We had no money, no place to stay, and no change of clothes. The situation would become more precarious if he noticed the car my father used to drive parked outside. "I'm not sure where we are staying yet. I can come back in a day or two and see where things stand, okay?"

As he rose to his feet, we followed suit, and he extended his hand. "Perfect. Meanwhile, I'll give your aunt a ring."

Dianne made her way to the door. Just as I turned to follow her, he interjected, "Cora, may I have a minute? Alone?"

My eyes flickered to Dianne's, and I gave her a subtle nod before she exited. Alone, he cautiously inquired, "I know it's not my place, but I need to ask. Are you okay? Is she... I mean you two look..." There was a pause. "I just need to know if I should worry. Do you need any help?"

At 18 years old, I didn't quite know how to respond to that question. These days, I might have politely hinted that it was none of his business. "No. I mean, we were on a trip with some friends, but it wasn't really working out, so we ventured off on our own and ended up here. I dropped by the old house, and the lady there mentioned you. That's all."

"You mentioned being between places. Running from St. Louis?" he probed.

"I wouldn't call it running, exactly. More like wanting a fresh start."

"Well, glad to know you are safe. Saw on the news they found a house full of dead bodies outside Tulsa. It's horrible. But, really. Do you need money? Food? A place to stay?" Before I could respond, he retrieved his wallet and handed me some bills. "If you need a safe space, let me know."

"Thanks, Mr. Jefferies." With a turn on my heel, I exited the office, with Dianne by my side.

Sloppy Joseph

Joseph Jefferies. Yes. He was a simple man, and once he sorted out my place of residence, financial affairs, and inheritance, Dianne killed him in the dead of night. The reason for his murder was not for food; it was because he was not a nice guy. I discovered Vera wasn't receiving the full amount from the property rental. Apparently, he had informed Vera that the rent for the house was 500 dollars a month, deducting 20 percent for managing the listing. The family paid him 750 dollars monthly. He pocketed the extra. Not only that, but he was shagging the secretary while being married, and he abused his wife. I'm pretty sure I remembered him creeping out of my sister's bedroom one late night when I should have been asleep, but memories from childhood are blurry.

Faced with everything we had learned the last few months, Dianne stalked him for almost a week before confronting him in his driveway, dragging him into our car, and ensuring his permanent disappearance. I knew what she had done when she came home that night with a plastic grocery bag filled with a hairy leg and asked for sloppy joes.

Ingredients

1 small onion, finely chopped

1/2 small green bell pepper, seeded and finely diced

1 tablespoon Worcestershire sauce

1 1/2 teaspoons yellow mustard

1 tablespoon brown sugar

15 ounce can tomato sauce

1 pound lean ground meat, 85%-90% lean (and if you can find someone named Joe, all the better)

1 tablespoon olive oil

1/2 teaspoon salt, or to taste

1/4 teaspoon ground black pepper, or to taste

3 garlic cloves, minced

1/4 cup water, optional, or added to desired consistency

4 hamburger buns

Instructions

- Finely chop the onion. Seed and finely dice the green pepper.

- In a bowl, combine the Worcestershire sauce, mustard, brown sugar, and tomato sauce and set to the side.

- Place a large skillet over medium-high heat. Add olive oil and ground meat. Sauté the meat for about five minutes until cooked through and no longer pink, breaking it up into little pieces with a spatula.

- Season with salt and pepper and add in the diced peppers and onion.

- Continue cooking for another five minutes until the veggies become tender and the meat browns.

- Add the minced garlic and sauté 30 seconds until fragrant, stirring constantly.

- Add in the sauce and bring to a light boil.

- Reduce heat to low and simmer uncovered for about 10-15 minutes or until thickened to your liking. Season to taste with salt and pepper and add water if you prefer a loose consistency. Serve on warm buns for Sloppy Joseph sandwiches.

Chapter 12

Leaving Oklahoma in a rush wasn't part of the plan, but the sudden police presence made it a necessity. Conversations were overdue, but speaking with Dianne was daunting. With Sadie or Abby, I wouldn't hesitate to confront or question them, but with Dianne, it felt different. There was a power imbalance between us, perhaps because of our age difference or a certain level of admiration mingled with apprehension.

Joseph Jefferies provided enough money for a motel and some basic clothing. We couldn't afford to be selective about our accommodations or attire. Yet, two pressing needs loomed: rest and sustenance. And there was an impending discussion that couldn't be put off.

Mid-afternoon found us on a stretch of road lined with a cluster of motels on the west side of town, each advertising affordable nightly rates. It took a few attempts to find one that would accommodate us without requiring identification. Dianne didn't have any, nor did I.

Inside the room, Dianne drew the curtains shut and collapsed onto the queen-size bed. In mere moments, she was fast asleep. I wasn't far behind her.

Sometime later, the light flooding in from outside and the creak of the door opening jolted me awake. Dianne had planned on slipping out of the room. "Where are you off to?" I mumbled, barely awake.

"Go back to sleep. I'll be back," she replied, not halting her steps.

I scrambled to my feet and hurried to the door, catching her arm as she attempted to close it. "Don't leave without me. I'm coming with you."

She hesitated, then relented. "Fine. Put your shoes on."

We strolled through the darkness, ducking into the shadows as we surveyed the neighborhood. Loitered with sex workers, they propositioned us many times; to all of which Dianne tossed up her hand and warded them off. The streets smelled of sex. Warm, hot, molten sex. Dianne picked up her pace as if a magnet drew her toward the scent. The aroma got stronger with each step.

Just as we turned a corner, a woman in a darkened alley stopped us. Behind her was an open trash bag. She wore a smile on her face, dressed in black like the night.

We both could smell the scent of fresh-killed human, but I held Dianne's hand tight, keeping her by my side.

"You're one of us. Need to feast?" asked the woman. It was as if she knew this body bag would attract the beasts like a vulture flying over wounded prey.

Dianne's greedy, salivating body vibrated and she growled out, "Yes. We both do."

A metallic blood scent muddled the air like a meat shoppe smoking barbecue. The scent of a freshly killed person hung in the air. I could almost taste it in the breeze. My hands gripped Dianne's waist, pulling me close to her like a bitch in heat.

"Ten dollars a person. All you can eat," she said.

Dianne looked at me for the money, but I hesitated. Even if I could smell our meal like cookies baking in an oven, I worried that this was some sort of trap to catch people like us. "We should talk about this first."

Drool pooled in the corners of her lips, dripping down as she opened her mouth to say words laced with such hunger: "Pay her the money."

I had never seen her eyes so needy, glowing in the darkness like rubies lit on fire. Or maybe I had because at that moment, I remembered Dianne in the bathroom of Hell Kitchen when my sister came out of the stall. That same look. Dianne was more than hungry for food; she needed sex.

Reluctantly, I pulled a bill out of my pocket and handed the 20 to this stranger, who then pulled open a steel door for us. Dianne tore forward, following the stench of death with hurried steps. I followed, but with a less fervent urgency. She took two steps at a time as she ascended the staircase that opened to a large room, more like an abandoned warehouse where groups of hungry women feasted on bloody carcasses on the floor. I lost Dianne within the sea of creatures, all with twisted expressions of primal, carnal lust.

Mouths biting into meat and organs, tearing it from the skinless torsos. Those who had already dined engaged in orgies to satisfy the other ravenous need.

The screams of a live woman pierced my ears, echoing against the brick walls. The deep howls of a man in pain rang in my ears. A man or burly woman dressed in a green rubber jumpsuit and boots had another woman in cuffs, dragging her naked body—kicking and screaming—to the dead center of the room. Before the server could even step out of the way, a throng of carnivorous women brutalized the horrified soul, each looking to be the victor in having her breasts or cunt first.

I had been so hypnotized by the sight before me I failed to notice the finely dressed woman who walked up next to me until she spoke. "Why are you not basking in the pleasures I have provided?"

With a shrug of my shoulders, I turned my attention back to the display in front of me. Dianne had ventured to this new woman. Her clothes were off, and her hands were on another human-eater while sinking her teeth into warm, gooey, rare meat. That might have been why I didn't partake so freely. If I joined them, it might not be Dianne who brought me pleasure but someone who I shared no emotional connection with. Despite the throbbing of my engorged clit, I only wanted Dianne's mouth on me.

This woman pushed me forward, though I wouldn't go. I didn't trust myself or anyone else in the room, including the one who seemed to run this underground meat market. Instead, I lowered myself to the floor, tucked my knees to my chest, and pleased myself while watching others lose what little self-control they had, including Dianne.

It didn't take long for these uncontrollable animals to consume the bodies beyond identification. And once they satiated both types of appetites, the feral creatures exited the building. With only a few of them left, I rose to my feet and walked over to one of the mangled corpses, just to pick up the part of her foot that someone had gnawed away from the rest of her body. I nibbled at the remaining meat, similar to how a dog would gnaw on a bone.

At that point, when the room had emptied, I noticed movement above me. I hadn't realized that one wall was only half-bricked with the top portion made of glass. A shuffle of people behind it resembled movie theater patrons leaving after the show. Stepping back again, I peered up, trying to focus my eyes on what lay above. Just then, I tossed the foot in the air, causing it to bounce against the glass wall. The eyes of everyone, mostly men, beyond the reflective surface, darted toward the noise. I could see the round, white faces looking down at us, and I realized we had a perverted audience.

In that moment, I exited the same way I had come in, passing the slow-moving, full-bellied zombies in a rush. As soon as I reached the street, my lungs opened up, and I caught a chest full of the summer night air. Maybe others didn't care about their exploits being gawked at, but I did. From the very beginning, there was an uneasy feeling about this. A feeding frenzy was too good to be true. Mad and scared, my blood boiled as I stormed away from the building.

Without waiting for Dianne, I sprinted down the street. Laughter echoed from an alley I passed. At the back door of the building, I spotted the woman who had urged me into that feverish debauchery, her evil smile fueling my rage like a jet engine. With each step, my hatred grew. I charged at her, my fist ready, and struck her square in the cheek. Blood spurted from her mouth as her head snapped to the side. I heard the crack of her jaw dislocating.

When I turned to walk away I heard a man's voice say, "She's a feisty one."

"The one who sat in the corner masturbating," said someone else, still behind my back.

Their words spun me around. Primal fury surged through me so fast that I tossed all restraint out the window. I was on the verge of lunging at them, ready to tear into their flesh with claws I didn't possess, when I felt a force pull me back. Firm hands gripped my shoulders, preventing me from unleashing my wrath and devouring them in a fit of anger.

Those hands belonged to Dianne, leaning in close. "Let's go," she urged, "and leave these people be."

She didn't understand. She didn't know what they had done. As the men strolled away in the opposite direction, toward the garage, Dianne ushered me away from them and the back door of the huge building. Before we could vanish entirely, the woman called out, "We'll see you next Friday?"

While Dianne's cravings may have subsided, the night left me with unfulfilled desires. Mine was the cold-blooded murder of that woman and those men who marveled at our disease, probably getting off to it like some kinky fetish.

As soon as we were far enough away from the building, I shook her hands off me. "Stop it. You're not my mother."

Suddenly, I no longer felt her near me. When I turned around, she had stopped walking and stood with her arms crossed in front of her. "You're right. I'm not your mother. I thought we put this past us."

I couldn't say anything because all I wanted to do was cry. Crawl into a hole and die. Instead of letting her see my pain, I shook my head and turned back around. I just wanted to go. Go anywhere. Away from life. Away from being a cannibal.

"What is your problem?"

That was it. Everything I had bottled up inside me for 11 long years came flying out of my mouth. All of it. "You. Her. This. You fucking killed my family. Ate them in front of me and I'm supposed to just go on living like nothing happened. Not talk about it? And you. You have been the only thing I have thought about this entire time. Some fucking obsession I have with you. And here you are... You won't touch me. You can barely even look at me. Off having sex while that woman and those guys were watching you. All of us. But you're too blind to see any of it because you're a monster. It's your fault I'm like this. It's your fault I'm alone. But you're so fucking blind to see that I'm right here!" My words softened as I started to cry. "I'm right here."

She hadn't really heard me. Or maybe I had just rambled so much that it had lost meaning. "Is that what this is about? You and me?"

"Why did you say no to me at the house? Tell me to stop and not to make love to you?"

She shook her head, pressing her lips together, then started walking again. When I didn't follow her, she flipped back around with her hand extended, as if she needed to protect me but her eyes didn't meet mine. "Are you coming?"

"Tell me why you can't bring yourself to look at me."

"Stop. Cora. Please. Let's just go back to the motel." Still her eyes didn't rise.

"No. Tell me. Why do you not want me?"

She paused. Probably more frustrated that I wouldn't stop asking. When I didn't move, she finally said, "Because you're still a child. You are still seven years old to me, and as much as I want you, I can't stop seeing that little girl. The fear in her eyes. I can still see that fear in your eyes now. Look, I'm sorry about your family. I am, but this is the reality of our life now. Trust me, I didn't want this for you and if I could turn back time, I would but here we are. Despite how easy you think it is, you're not the one who wants 18-year-old Cora naked but can only see that child in front of me. My mind can't reconcile the difference."

It made sense. But I wasn't that child anymore. I may not have killed yet, but I had feasted on flesh—both literally and figuratively. I was a woman; and I wanted her. With slow, precise steps, I walked to her and pressed my body into hers. Her head tilted away from me, like an internal struggle between right and wrong. The palm of my hand pressed her cheek, and I forced her to look at me. "I'm not seven."

"I know." Her words got caught in the summer breeze and drifted away as our lips met for the first time.

Tenderloin with Roasted Figs

Let's just take sex to an entirely new level here. A tenderloin with roasted figs. Yes! Figs are fascinating, symbolically, because the fruit itself has a notorious, historical representation of sensuality, while its leaves represent modesty. Clearly, there is a complex virgin/whore complex going on with this fruit. I'm sure you'd agree.

In biblical times, Eve wore fig leaves to cover her tenderloin. The fig's exterior is testicular looking, while the inside suggests the female sex organ. Plus, the fig was purportedly Cleopatra's favorite food, so it's got some potential power. And in ancient Greece, a new fig crop always led to a sexual ritual.

Did you know artists incorporated figs into many paintings, some of which depicted infants under a fig tree, where they were being nursed by a she-wolf? The Romans also associated the fig tree with Rumina, patron goddess of breastfeeding mothers, because of its milky sap. With so many innuendos tied to figs, it was impossible for me not to create a dish with a woman's tenderloin.

For the tenderloin, slice up into the center of the woman's sex, then cut around the curve between the inner thigh and groin, and slide the knife as close to the femur as possible, down to the knee. You want the inner meat area. Repeat on the other side of the body.

Ingredients

3 cloves garlic, minced

2 teaspoons finely chopped fresh rosemary, plus 2 big sprigs

1 tablespoon Dijon mustard

2 teaspoons pure maple syrup

1 teaspoon kosher salt, plus more if needed

Freshly ground black pepper

Two 1 to 1-1/4-pound tenderloins

1 tablespoon extra-virgin olive oil, divided

16 fresh figs

1 tablespoon balsamic vinegar, divided

Instructions

- Two or more hours before cooking starts: In a small bowl mix the garlic, rosemary, Dijon mustard, maple syrup, salt, and several healthy cracks of black pepper from a pepper grinder.

- Use your hands to coat the two tenderloins with the

marinade. If you are marinating the loin, a few hours ahead of time, wrap and refrigerate.

- Preheat oven to 400 degrees. Allow an extra 30 minutes to rest at temperature before adding meat to oven.

- Remove the loin from the refrigerator a half hour before cooking.

- Just before cooking, season the outside of the tenderloins with an additional 1/2 teaspoon kosher salt. Heat two teaspoons of the oil over high heat in an oven-proof skillet large enough to comfortably accommodate both tenderloins.

- Add the meat to the pan and cook on all sides until nicely browned. Meat does not need to be cooked thoroughly.

- While the meat is browning, toss the figs in a medium bowl with the remaining one teaspoon of oil, one teaspoon of balsamic vinegar and a pinch of salt.

- Once you brown the meat, add the figs and rosemary sprigs to the pan and put it in the oven.

- Cook until done. The time will vary depending on the thickness of the tenderloin. Test for doneness by inserting an instant-read thermometer in the center of the thickest part of the loin. For pinker and more tenderloin, remove it at 140 to 145 degrees. For a more well-done finish, cook until 150 to 155 degrees. This will take approximately 20 minutes.

- Remove the pan from the oven and transfer the meat to a carving board. Let it rest for at least five minutes.

- Cut the meat crosswise into 1/2-inch thick slices and arrange on a platter with the figs.

- With the drippings in the pan, add the remaining two teaspoons of balsamic vinegar and stir it together. Drizzle these pan drippings over the meat and figs, season with more salt and fresh black pepper to your liking and serve immediately.

Chapter 13

You might think we went back to the motel and hooked up, right? Were you rooting for us? Saying "yes" with a giant fist pump. Sorry to disappoint you, but we did not. I gave her time to process my presence. Even though we had been together for a while now, I understood that she needed to see me for me, as an adult. If we were meant to be, it would come with time.

Over the next week, Joseph Jefferies helped me secure identification and set up a bank account so that I could start receiving money. There were still many hoops to jump through, and it would take time for the filed paperwork to pass through the courts. He deposited a small allowance for me to survive during the wait.

I experienced a wave of relief as I realized that, at least for the time being, I was not a person of interest in any police investigations related to events in Oklahoma when the found William and Abby's bodies. I had mentioned to Vera that I separated from them prior to that, which everyone accepted as the truth. Dianne wasn't confident in her situation. Even living off the grid, there was always the possibility the police had footage, photographs, or something to link her to that house where there were at least three dead bodies shut in a freezer.

Over the years, she had murdered many people at that diner for sustenance. Come to find out, when the pig lady attempted to molest and eat Sadie one night, Dianne killed her. That was when Dianne decided Sadie needed more protection. From her. From everyone. To do that, she fed her human meat until the smell of her sex no longer penetrated the air. She had prayed I had consumed none of the food that night at the diner, but when Sadie had found me and told Dianne of my disease, it saddened her as well as relieved her.

The problem of food persisted for us. What Dianne had eaten that night satisfied her for a while, but after a week without proper meals, we both needed something to quell the growing discomfort in our stomachs. It wasn't just hunger. We saw things that weren't there. That's how it begins. Without human flesh, the mind plays tricks on us. This is why Robert turned into a wolf shifter during sex. Tyson's great white shark mouth wanted to chomp down on my lower extremities. It wasn't just sexual. One ant turned into a million and my mind thought they were crawling in my mouth to suffocate me. There were others but in order for the hallucinations to stop, we needed to eat human meat.

We hadn't planned to stay in New Mexico indefinitely, nor did we have concrete plans to leave. The motel wasn't a permanent solution.

We searched for a more stable place to stay, at least until the lease expired on my parents' home, giving us the option to move in if we decided to. Our relationship, Dianne's and mine, remained stalled. Instead of acting upon her desires, she masturbated behind a closed bathroom door while I satisfied myself in bed without her.

When Friday arrived, marking a solid week since we had last eaten. Dianne came out of the bathroom, dressed and scrubbed up. I was still in bed, basking in my afterglow, when she said, "I'm going out."

I shot up; the blanket slipped down from my frame, dropping onto my lap. The cool air in the room perked my nipples, which I wasn't afraid to show her. "Without me? Where are you going?"

"I need to eat, Cora," she stated flatly.

"We both need to eat!" I insisted. "I can help search for someone."

Frustrated, she shook her head. "I'm going back to that place."

We hadn't discussed it since our argument. While it might have been a place to grab a bite to eat like a fast-food joint, there were hazards to it. Hazards such as voyeurs who got off to watching women act like savages. "You can't go there. It's not safe."

"It's better than chancing an area I don't know. Cora, it's not as easy as running outside and killing someone," she said, then added, "you saw what happened to Sadie. If I can pay to eat then I would rather do that."

By that point, I was out of bed standing with no clothes on and my hands on my hips. "Then I'm coming with you."

Returning to this lust-infested, all-you-can-eat food and sex buffet wasn't my idea of a good time, or the wisest of ideas. At the door, we paid the cover charge again, and before I knew it, Dianne had taken off to feast on her carnal desires despite my protests. She cared not that there were onlookers, people enjoying the exploitation show of barbaric women. Much like last time, there were piles of bodies. A male's torso on the floor in a mangled lump of grizzly carnage. The one reason I knew it was a male was from the hairy leg, much thicker than the average woman's. As the flesh-eating carnivores tore away pieces of him, I noticed that his male appendage was no longer there, much like his face and stomach area.

Over the years, I found out that there wasn't much difference between the two sexes. Most cannibals didn't care who they consumed, which I learned throughout the years. You picked the easiest person to kill and chow time. Meat was meat and sat on a plate in front of you, you eat. Over time, I came to realize there were nuances. Like an oyster connoisseur, I could effortlessly identify the distinctions in origin. To the average seafood eater, it's just a slimy mass of salty snot. That was how men tasted to me before I began cooking full time. But at that moment, in that hour of need, I picked up a tossed-away bone and suckled as much of the meat away from it as I could.

Throughout the evening, my attention shifted between the multitude of dinner guests and the observation deck, which I concluded was just a pornography live theater where viewers, mostly males, jerked off to the show. There was one woman up there, bouncing on their laps with her tits jiggling up and down. When she finished one person, she moved to the next and repeated. The entire ordeal nauseated me. I wanted to vomit at the sight of it all, but I needed to eat, which I did.

Most of the women partaking in the feeding frenzy also engaged in the sexual freedom allowed to them. I don't think everyone in the room was a lesbian. No, they were like any horny mammal. They humped anything with a pulse. Despite my sex feeling like a lamprey sucking the air and driving me toward another warm body, I resisted.

As I looked back up to the deck, I spotted the woman from the last encounter—the one I confronted in the alley. Our eyes locked in a tense stare-down. However, a squishy noise caught my attention, causing me to turn away from her. Dianne had tossed me a literal bone.

When my eyes returned upward, the woman was gone. I caught sight of her when she entered the lower level from a side door. Dressed in a pair of jeans and a blazer, she strolled over to me with an arrogant smirk.

"You're not like them, are you?" she asked.

"Not sure what you mean by that, but I am." I held up my bone and took a hefty bite from it.

"There are two things that come from this disease. A hefty appetite, and well, a hefty appetite. You seem to only have one of those."

"And you know this how?" I asked.

"Tell me something. Why are you not enjoying yourself?"

Did my scowl give it away? I answered her, "Because I'm not proud to be here, let alone with the eyes of people who clearly aren't living like scavengers on me."

"You're pretty young to have such a big theory on the matter."

"Young, but not stupid. If this is your place, how much money are they paying you to sit up there and jerk off at *them*?" I pointed to the mass of fucking bodies in front of us.

She leaned close to me, almost whispering in my ear. "It's more than money they are providing." When she stepped back, she continued, "Money keeps the lights on, rent paid, and the cops away. It doesn't keep food on the table. That's an entirely different negotiation. You should appreciate the charity they are offering to you."

"Is that what you call this? Charity?" My body totally shifted around, facing her instead of the masses behind me. My fists clenched, and I tensed my muscles, ready to drive them forward.

Instead of seeing my rage, she placed her arm over my shoulder and nudged me with her. "I like you and your spunk. We should talk more, and away from all this—and those prying eyes."

I had a gut feeling that things were about to take a turn for the worse. And I'm almost sure you're shouting at the page, telling me not to go with her. Am I right? So was Dianne, who ran toward me as I was about to step behind the iron curtain of this joint.

"Hey. Whoa. Wait!" Dianne's body glistened with a crimson hue, covered in a mixture of blood and entrails. Her hand pulled at mine, like a tug-of-war for my person against a woman we didn't even know.

My hand slid away from her soaked palm as the woman dragged me through and shut the door, leaving Dianne on the other side. She led me to a room that resembled a lounge, with a sofa and a few chairs. She sat down, gesturing for me to join her. I hesitated, then settled on the sofa opposite her. Her arms draped over the arms of her chair. She crossed her legs and leaned back.

"What's your name, kid?" she asked.

My throat swelled up, making it very hard to breathe. "Cora," I barely eked out.

"Colleen Marnoff. How old are you?"

My cockiness got lost somewhere between the warehouse floor and this plush room. My voice cracked. "Eighteen."

From there, she asked me about how I came to learn about our sickness, and she shared the story of her infection. Every question she asked led to a tale of her life. Much of our lives, and maybe all the others', were quite the same. What I realized while talking to her is that we all shared this, but no one wanted to talk about it. Dianne, who knew how I got changed, never told me about her journey. I knew more about Colleen than I knew about the woman I loved.

When she asked me again why I hadn't partaken in the deviant aspect of fulfilling that primal urge, I said, "Because I'm in love with that woman, and I don't want anyone else touching me."

"Have you considered she may *not* be a lesbian? Not all of us enjoy being with women. I don't. I much prefer riding a giant cock for a few hours," she said, with no filter.

It made me laugh, lightening the mood in the room. "She is; it's just that we have a sordid past which includes her eating my sister in more ways than one."

"We all have our crosses to bear. Here are the facts of all this…"

Colleen was an older woman, probably in her forties, and had been living this way for more years than I had been alive. I figured I might as well listen because she seemed to have a handle on living with this disease without turning into a ferocious feral beast.

"As long as I can keep the infected women fed, the city is safe. With the help of my associates, we bring in people who have… gone off the grid, so to speak. Let's just say we have a well-oiled machine that provides us with food. Because of this, Albuquerque doesn't have unexplained murders, no wild cannibals running through the streets. We search out people like us and take care of those we can. Trust me, I will kill those who choose to prey on their own terms. I will not sugarcoat this, Cora. It's my way or the highway. Your options are simple: accept the reality that rich men *and women* who indulge in unconventional fetishes support your safety, or get the hell out of my town."

I gave her a nod, then stood up. As I reached for the door to leave, I asked, "What do you do with the bodies after we've picked them over?"

"I dispose of them. Circle of life. We give our leftovers to the wolves, coyotes, and vultures."

"Can I have them? Or parts of them?"

"Why?"

"There's still enough there for me to cook; we wouldn't have to wait another week to eat again," I said, still with my hand on the door.

There was a pause. "You cook humans?"

"Yeah."

Again, there was a pause. When I turned around, I saw her scribbling something down on a business card, then she handed it to me. At first, I glanced at the front of it: Colleen Marnoff. Marnoff Companies, Inc. On the back was an address. A puzzled look crossed my face.

"Be there at seven in the morning tomorrow. Let's see how well you can cook." She winked at me. Then, I pressed out the door and back to where most of the women had already feasted on the pleasures of flesh.

Dianne had not moved from the door, so when I came out, she checked me over in a panic. "Are you okay? What happened? Where did you go?"

"I'm fine." Maybe what Colleen said had resigned me to the fact that Dianne and I would never be, but my sarcasm and animosity slithered out in my words. "Are you satisfied enough to go home yet, or do you need to go snack on some more snatch?"

I didn't wait for her to answer. Instead, I bounded away and down the outside stairs, leaving the building to find my way back to the motel.

Before morning, Dianne returned to the motel, tiptoeing into the room. I shouldn't have been mad at her then, or even the night before, but I was. The increasing anger I felt might have been because spending time with her, and also being around the temptations of the bestial feast, made me a walking hormone.

Still a girl in love, I blew up as soon as the door closed. "Why are you still even here? You don't love me. You won't touch me, or even talk to me. There's nothing you want here, so just go away."

She wasn't much for conversation, often lost in the weight of her own troubles. My words didn't divert her course to the bathroom, though this time, she didn't shut the door behind her. Her clothes dropped onto the bed as she crossed the room, landing on top of me. Positioned there, I could subtly watch her movements through the angled mirrors. Much like a stalker, my eyes remained fixed on her. I had a very unhealthy fixation on this woman.

Perhaps we both felt it, because when she pivoted, our eyes locked within the mirror's frame. Her back straightened and her chest rose, still caked with a dried burgundy layer of blood. Neither of us moved, as if she was daring me to enter. After a moment I stood up and edged closer, moving just inside the doorway. Still, she held her ground.

The shower water was beyond hot enough for her to have stepped into the tub, but there she was: naked and radiating a heat that I hadn't felt in her before. It was as if her body was an inferno. Still, she didn't move. I stepped in front of her, just inches away from her, but I didn't touch. I only wanted to inhale her musky stench of death and arousal.

She couldn't let me be. No, she reached for my hand and pressed it against her sex. There might have been a brief resistance from me, but I didn't tear myself away from her. My fingers slipped between her folds, finding a searing pool of her lust and her engorged clit. I hadn't had my hands on her for a second before the weight of her body backed me against the wall. She tore at my pajamas, pulling down my pants and reaching between my legs with a fever so intense I lost track of my own abilities. Her mouth covered mine, taking my breath away as her fingers swirled over my clit with such vigor and power, like a Kitchen Aid mixer on high. I moaned inside her mouth, which she devoured like candy. When those coos of pleasure turned to shrieks of euphoria, she reached even lower and pressed her fingers up into my sex. It felt as if my feet no longer touched the ground. I burst around her fingers, sending a river of warmth over her hand. Never in my life had I come so hard as I did then. Yet, she didn't let me go. When my body melted like butter in her arms, she guided me into the shower, where she licked every inch of me until I could no longer stand on my own.

Liver and Onions

As I was putting this book together, I left some open space in which I could include some dishes that might go nowhere else within my story but are essential to being a cannibal. As always, we need to use all the pieces of the human body. While the most obvious pieces are the meat itself, how about those entrails?

A recipe for using those scraps of a body would be the classic liver dish. It might be difficult to look at someone and decide if their liver is healthy. If you are a fan of healthy eating, I would recommend not looking for your next meal at a bar. Despite being the most logical spot for a hook-up and the perception that those who go there are easy targets... do your homework. If you do prefer to hunt at bars, though, stake out a few different locations. Pay attention to who's frequenting them. If you find a specific person at one place often, skip them. First, if they don't show up, someone will notice their absence. Two, their liver is probably shot. This is the one part of the body you don't want fatty.

I normally love a girl with a little junk in the trunk. A little excess fat is a good thing. But not on liver. As much as we love fresh insides, a fatty liver will leave a sour taste on your tongue.

For this recipe, you only need one human liver. Inside the average person, a liver weighs about three pounds. With your meat scale, measure it out. Save the extra for the Brunswick stew (page: 51).

Ingredients

2 pounds liver, cut into 4 steaks

2 tablespoons unsalted butter

1 large yellow onion, sliced into 1/4-inch slices

Kosher salt

Black pepper

1/2 cup whole milk

1 large egg

2 cups breadcrumbs

2 tablespoons vegetable oil

Instructions

- Place the liver in a mixing bowl. Cover with water and let it soak for 15 to 20 minutes. This will remove any toxins that may be present. Kind of like erasing the sour taste.

- In a large cast-iron skillet, melt the butter over medium-low heat.

- Add the onions and cook while stirring occasionally, until tender and lightly browned. Remove from the skillet and season to taste with salt.

- In a shallow bowl, whisk together the milk and eggs until well blended. Place the breadcrumbs on a plate.

- Rinse the liver under cool running water and then pat dry with paper towels. Lightly season each side with salt and pepper.

- Dip into the milk mixture, then into the breadcrumbs, coating evenly.

- Pour the oil into the skillet that you used for the onions and turn the heat to medium heat.

- After the oil has heated, add the liver, and cook for two to three minutes on each side or until cooked through. Top with the onions.

- And lastly... enjoy!

Chapter 14

Just as I was about to fall asleep in my euphoric bliss, Dianne nudged me away from her in bed and then pulled herself out. I asked, "Where are you going?"

"To shower," she replied, as if we hadn't just been there a few hours earlier.

"Again?"

"I smell like you," she said and added, "as much as I'd like to stay like this, you have an appointment to get to."

My neck twisted, and I glanced at the clock. It was seven in the morning, and yes, I had an appointment at eight, though I wasn't planning to go, not now. Not after my dreams of being with Dianne had come true. What puzzled me at that moment was the fact that she knew about it. It wasn't like I had told her when I left the warehouse after meeting Colleen.

With that knowledge, I rose on my elbows, giving her a side-eyed glare. "How do you know about that?"

"That woman is very smitten with you," Dianne said as she turned on the bathroom faucet, heating the water. There was something else she said, but I didn't hear it over the shower water. When I got out of bed and followed her into the bathroom, I heard her say, "This is something you need to do."

"What did she say to you?" I asked, leaning on the frame as she stripped down to nothing.

"That I'm an idiot. Then she asked if you cooked for me."

"What did you say?"

"I agreed with her about being an idiot." She stepped forward and reached out just enough to touch my stomach. "I'm afraid of losing you. Again."

The last word was so soft, I barely heard it. Her eyes still held a sadness as I gazed into them. My hand lifted to her cheek, then ran through her feathered, dirty blonde hair. When it came around to the back of her head, I pulled her toward me and lifted myself to reach her lips. We kissed so softly.

"You will not lose me."

"You say that now." There was doubt in her voice.

"I'll say that always."

Our rusty old station wagon pulled up in front of the iron gates of a French country ranch home nestled in the Sandia Mountains. The view from the secluded street was magnificent. The enormous house sat farther off the drive, visible up the winding path.

An armed guard stationed at the gate stepped to the car window. He glanced over at us, disdain clear for our worn-out vehicle. His hand rested on his gun, showing off its size. My gaze shifted to the stone wall encircling the residence while Dianne handed him my identification. Another man, wielding an assault rifle, sat atop the wall.

When he requested Dianne's identification, she shook her head, stating she didn't have any. He seemed unwilling to grant us entry until I intervened. "Colleen is expecting us. Call her if you need verification."

He conversed with the guard, casting a scrutinizing glance into our vehicle. Their exchange was in a foreign language that sounded like Spanish but held some noticeable differences. I later discovered it was Brazilian Portuguese. Soon, the gate opened, granting us entry behind this iron curtain. Our car moved forward and settled into the expansive parking area in front of the residence. The pebbled drive resembled a parking lot filled with various Hummers and Jeeps, their windows tinted.

As we emerged from our car, the front door swung open to reveal Colleen, dressed in a Japanese kimono, her hair tied back neatly. It was a stark contrast to the stern business attire she had worn at the warehouse. Her smile now offered a warm welcome, a far cry from the tough facade of the previous night.

"Welcome! I'm delighted you've joined me. After the way you left last night, I half-expected not to see you again. Come in. Let's have a chat before we get started," Colleen said, stepping aside to usher us in.

The two-story foyer greeted us with antique wooden tables and a sideboard, and with a large iron chandelier suspended from the ceiling. A vase filled with bright gerbera daisies added a vibrant splash of color to the beige-themed decor. It wasn't what I had expected her home to look like, but then again, I wasn't entirely certain of my expectations. Colleen guided us to a sitting room at the rear of the house, equipped with double French doors that opened to a spacious indoor pool area. Out in that area were gorgeous, naked men, stallions with muscular-framed bodies and cocks to match. They bathed under the glass frame that allowed the morning sun to brighten the area.

When my eyes spent more time questioning the naked guys walking around, Colleen said, "I told you I appreciated a well-hung bull. Come on, let's sit."

Dianne and I settled into the offered seats. I chose a position where I could avoid being distracted by others.

"I had anticipated you'd come alone," Colleen remarked, casting a sidelong glance at Dianne. "But, this is fine—"

Dianne interjected, "She doesn't drive, and well, I wasn't entirely comfortable letting her come alone."

The conversation took a suggestive turn. "From what I heard, you don't let her come at all. Now, back to the reason she..." Her attention shifted to me. "You are here. Food. Before this disease nearly killed me, I indulged in some of the most exquisite dishes. Some of the finest cuts of meat, enjoyed at some of the world's most prestigious restaurants. And then, well, it all changed. Any meat I put into my stomach made me vomit. Do you know how disheartening it is to regurgitate Japanese Wagyu beef that costs 200 dollars per pound?"

She paused, as if waiting for a response. At that point in my life, I wasn't even sure what Wagyu beef was. The thought of it now, well... Yes, it is downright tragic.

When we said nothing, she continued. "No matter what I ate, I lost weight. I was close to death, though I was very much alive with an overactive sex drive. It wasn't until my nail dug into my lover's chest during my eagerness that I realized what cured my illness. To his dismay, I ate him. Alive! When I scratched open his stomach, I pulled out all of his intestines and devoured as much of him as I could in one sitting. The next morning, I returned to him and continued without a second thought. I'm sure you've both had similar experiences."

We both nodded as she continued. "Here is our situation. My family and lovers are unaware of our misfortune. If they knew, they'd consider me a threat, and the consequences wouldn't be favorable. Their survival depends on my ability to stay fed. I have enlisted some... business associates to provide our necessity. However, I miss the simple pleasures of food—sitting at a table with fine wine and a plate of delicacies. Right now, my food intake is much like yours. Because I keep my infection a secret, I'm relegated to eating in the barn like the other animals. To find someone who can cook... or should I say *willing* to cook human meat, I believe I can extend my support in return for your aid."

Again, there was a long pause hanging over us. A silence that allowed me to understand exactly what she wanted from me. "So instead of giving me the leftovers, so to speak, you want me to cook them for you?"

"Let's just say we would both win."

"How so?"

"I don't know many people. Let me start over. I don't know anyone who can, or will, cook a human being and not feel disgusted by the thought. I can threaten my staff with their lives, but I don't trust them enough to know my secret will remain a secret."

That's when Dianne spoke up. "How much of this is a secret when you have run an underground cannibal club?"

As Colleen switched legs, crossing one over the other, a man entered the room. She gestured to silence us until he exited. "I'm worth half a billion dollars. The family, even more. I'm serving the community by keeping this disease under control. I prefer to keep my situation private from everyone except one specific person. I think we all have that one person, a confidant to scratch each other's backs."

"So, how do we benefit?" I gestured to show that Dianne was integral to my involvement, signaling that any benefit for me would extend to her, too.

Colleen stood up and beckoned for us to follow her. We walked through the house as if we were guests on a tour. She showcased her home, including the empty equestrian center with vacant stalls. Not once did she mention her plans, only highlighting her wealth. When we returned to the house, we entered through the back into a state-of-the-art, expansive kitchen. "You like to cook? Cook. Let's have breakfast. I've given my kitchen staff the morning off, so you'll have the run of the place. There are a few pieces of meat in the refrigerator and pretty much all the food and spices you'd want. I'll leave you two alone." Colleen tapped the wall near a buzzer. "Call me when breakfast is ready. I'll be out by the pool getting massaged."

Dianne leaned on the island as I inspected the kitchen. The fridge held a plethora of foods. Much like when Vera returned with groceries, I assessed what options they gave me and struck up a plan of action. An entire drawer contained a treasure chest of spices, ones I couldn't even pronounce. With minimal experience in cooking, other than winging it, I opened a few jars and took a sniff. The saffron, when I opened it, had a distinct aroma that urged me to use it. I had Dianne take a whiff, but she turned up her nose, although I knew I needed to incorporate it.

For the next hour, I mixed and cooked ingredients into a skillet stew, using the saffron and the meat she provided in a butcher-wrapped package. When I thought it was ready, I offered Dianne a taste.

"You really have a knack for this," she remarked.

"Maybe it's something I can do. I mean, we are going to need money, and I probably need to get a job soon," I said, shrugging. It was the first time I even considered the possibility of being a cook of some sort. Carefully, I cracked two eggs and poached them in the simmering sauce. Then I pressed the call button. I expected to hear a buzz or a ring, but there was no sound. We exchanged puzzled looks until Colleen entered the room, her kimono open with nothing underneath. The woman had no shame.

At the small cafe table in the bay window, I presented her with a dish concocted from whatever I could find that I thought would go together. She scooped a spoonful into her mouth, a mix of meat, eggs, cooked peas, saffron, and a multitude of spices. The sound of pleasure that escaped her mouth made her eyes roll backward.

"If I wasn't straight, I'd eat this right off your body and fuck you at the same time." She shoveled a few more heaping helpings into her mouth before she said, "Where did someone so young learn how to cook like this?"

"Necessity," I said.

"No training?"

"No."

"Do you want training?" she asked, the fullness of her mouth causing some to drip from the corners of her lips as she spoke.

"I don't have the money for cooking school," I replied.

"But I do." She pointed to the chair across from her. "Sit! You asked how you'd benefit from this. I trust you to keep your mouth shut. I'll employ you as my personal chef. You'll travel around the world, studying under the masters. Learn techniques, cuisines, cultures. Then you will come back here and figure out how to incorporate our special ingredient into these dishes. I'll provide you with whatever cuts you need, and you will feed me. It's a double win."

Sitting in the impressive kitchen, facing a woman who hadn't bothered to close her kimono and had her breasts barely covered, wasn't what I had expected from this meeting. All I had wanted was some leftovers from the club, so I could prepare a few small meals for Dianne and me during the week. I didn't know how to respond because it sounded too good to be true. Just a week ago, I wanted to harm this woman. Now, there was a job offer on the table that could effectively stop our weekly starvation.

Before I could agree, I glanced at Dianne, who remained standing at the island, giving Colleen her space. She nodded at me. I pressed my lips together, then asked, "What about her?"

My eyes returned to Colleen, who smirked. "If you say yes, I'll allow you this bodyguard. Your human pit bull to do your dirty work."

Though I disliked Colleen's view of Dianne as nothing more than a feral animal lacking grace, I agreed to her proposition. We sealed the deal with a handshake. Then she led us to a separate section of the equestrian center and opened a stall. In the corner, chains held a naked bound woman on the ground. Her head was split with dried blood caked in her hair. She squirmed as Colleen picked up a large chef's knife and entered.

She presented it to me and said, "And as your starting bonus, this one is for you. Do whatever you want to her, and when you're finished, cook. I'd like lunch around noon and dinner at five."

My jaw dropped. There were no words for what Colleen had given me—us, Dianne and me. This bound Hispanic woman was everything we could have wanted, ready and ripe for the taking. She'd be our next few meals, but in the meantime, I needed Dianne to have a go at me instead of this woman. I pressed my hands into her cheeks, forcing her eyes on me.

With my tongue, I licked the drool from her mouth, then said, "Take me."

And she did. Right there. On the dirt. In front of this woman, who I stabbed with the knife during my orgasm.

Thigh & Belly Paella

Over the years, I attempted to replicate the dish I created for Colleen on that summer morning, and the closest resemblance I could find was a paella. This Spanish dish derives its name from the wide, shallow pan used to cook it over an open fire, as "paella" signifies a frying pan in the Valencian/Catalan language. Ideally, a Spaniard could offer the most authentic rendition, yet the variety of spices and ingredients involved may obscure the essence of farm-raised Spanish meat.

Ingredients

1/2 teaspoon saffron threads

3 1/4 cups light broth (page: 23), divided

1 tablespoon olive oil

6 ounces dry-cured belly (page: 19), cut into 1/4-inch-thick slices

1 pound boneless, skinless thigh meat, cut into 1 1/2-inch pieces

1/2 teaspoon black pepper

1 1/2 teaspoons kosher salt, divided

3/4 cup chopped yellow onion (from 1 small onion)

1 small red bell pepper, finely chopped

4 small garlic cloves, minced (1 tablespoon)

1/2 teaspoon smoked paprika

1 (14 1/2-ounce) can diced tomatoes, undrained

1 1/2 cups uncooked short-grain white rice (such as Spanish bomba or Italian arborio)

1 cup thawed frozen sweet peas

Chopped fresh flat-leaf parsley, for garnish

Lemon wedges, for garnish

Instructions

- Gather the ingredients.

- Stir together saffron and 1/4 cup of the broth in a small bowl. Let stand at room temperature for at least 15 minutes, up to one hour.

- Meanwhile, heat oil in a 12-inch cast-iron skillet over medium-high. Add belly meat; cook, stirring occasionally, until lightly browned, about two minutes. Using a slotted spoon, transfer belly meat to a plate lined with paper towels; reserve drippings in a skillet.

- Add thigh meat, black pepper, and one teaspoon of the salt to the skillet; cook over medium-high, stirring occasionally, until lightly browned but not fully cooked, about seven minutes. Using a slotted spoon, transfer thigh to plate with belly. Do not wipe the skillet clean.

- Using the oils from the meat, add onion and bell pepper to the skillet; cook over medium-high, stirring occasionally, until tender, about five minutes.

- Stir in garlic and smoked paprika; cook, stirring constantly, until fragrant, about one minute.

- Mix in tomatoes and rice, cook while stirring until liquid is almost completely absorbed, about two minutes.

- Carefully stir in saffron mixture and remaining three cups broth and 1/2 teaspoon salt; bring to a simmer over medium-high heat.

- Return both meats to skillet, stirring lightly to partially cover with rice; sprinkle mixture with peas (do not stir peas in).

- Keep cooking uncovered and undisturbed over medium-low heat, occasionally rotating the skillet to disperse heat, until the chicken and rice become tender and the liquid is almost fully absorbed, which should take about 20 minutes.

- Remove from heat; cover and let stand at room temperature for about five minutes. Garnish with parsley and lemon wedges.

Notes:

For a breakfast with a twist, add one or two eggs to the dish right after removing it from the heat. The residual warmth from the pan and the meal will gently poach the eggs as the mixture cools down. By the time you're ready to eat, the eggs will be a delectable complement to the dish.

Chapter 15

It's fascinating how life unfolds. Some endure a perpetual struggle, striving for their slice of the pie. Others witness the stars aligning at that precise instant, fortunate enough to have things fall into place. Perhaps I was simply in the right place at the right time, finding myself blessed as Colleen Marnoff handed me the world on a silver platter. Believe me, that silver spoon wasn't an expected part of my narrative. I was an orphan plagued by an incurable disease, forced further into the unimaginable with each passing day.

Colleen's offer was indeed genuine. She hired me and funded my culinary education. It involved early mornings at her place before the sun rose over the Sandia Mountains. I'd handle the overnight-delivered meat and whip up an extravagant breakfast in a cramped kitchen with minimal ventilation. I wasn't in the main kitchen but a small one in a guest house close to the horse stables. Then, I'd dash across town for cooking lessons with an executive chef at a prestigious restaurant. I wasn't cooking human there but it taught me techniques and flavor pairings. Afterward, back at the compound, I'd prepare Colleen's lunch, only to rush back to the restaurant for another lesson. Finally, I'd return home and attempt to replicate the day's creations for Colleen's dinner using the meat from whomever we had in my private refrigerator.

That was my life, seven days a week. Remember those old folks who gripe about walking five miles to school uphill, in 10 feet of snow? What they don't tell you is that they probably lived in a gracious home, dined on a banquet, had loving parents, and drove fancy cars. That was not my reality. My days were a blend of vigorous schedules and strict routines. The pay, however, was more than any typical 18-year-old could dream of earning. With Dianne's help, we secured an apartment between both locations, and I bought a car that wasn't a rolling billboard advertising my family's tragedy.

Colleen allowed me to bring any extra food home, leftovers to be exact; and I could nibble while hacking away at some trafficked body. So, in the grand scheme of my culinary growth, I was doing well for myself.

At the start of the new year, the lease on my family's house was up for renewal, and I faced a choice: either evict the tenants or let them stay and keep collecting rent. After much debate with Dianne, we opted to evict them. The apartment lacked the privacy we craved, and while society was becoming more accepting of lesbian relationships, the openness wasn't there in the eighties. Especially not with our significant age gap of 16 years. There was no mistaking that she wasn't my mother or sister; our appearances were complete opposites.

Initially, stepping back into my childhood home felt surreal. I moved almost instinctively towards what used to be my bedroom, as if it were still mine. While examining the place, I noticed a series of notches on the door frame, marked with dates and my name beside them. The subsequent family had kept up the tradition, adding their own set of dates and the name of a person I'd never know. Dianne trailed her finger over my last entry, just a few days before my seventh birthday in 1977. When I tried to kiss her, she withdrew. It seemed like the place had stirred memories she'd rather leave in the past.

By this point, we'd been living together for six months, sharing not just the same space but also the same bed. Despite hauling in some thrift store furniture to furnish our new home, it didn't quite fill the entire house. As I surveyed the place, I couldn't help but notice the empty rooms, two bedrooms left unoccupied.

Something struck me about the situation. Since our arrival at this new residence, Dianne had made no kind of advance toward me, like we had regressed to when she still thought of me as a helpless child. It led me to pose a question: "Do you think we should get another bed and have separate rooms?"

She remained silent, her melancholia just beneath the surface. We'd completed most of the moving during the night—primarily because it was the only time I had available. There wasn't much of an opportunity to press the issue, so when it came time for work, I left. Returning later that day, it was well into the evening. I'd been awake for over 24 hours by then and collapsed on the sofa as soon as my body stopped racing.

During the months of this schedule, whenever I dozed off on the sofa, Dianne would usually carry me to bed. I'd wake up snug under the covers. This time, I awoke on the sofa in a darkened room. Something had shifted.

There was no room for arguments when Colleen put me on a truck bound for Mexico. Despite my protests, Dianne's protests, and my attempts to quit the job, I ended up on the other side of the border in a home where no one spoke English. My task was to learn as much about Mexican cuisine as I could from a woman I couldn't understand.

On my first day at this home, I spent it doing nothing but pressing out tortillas by hand and cooking them on a fire pit with a giant metal plate on top. I might have made a thousand of them, all of which turned out wrong—either too thick or too thin. Trust me, there's an art form for making tortillas. As much as I protested that it was easier to just buy them from the store, my words fell on deaf ears. This grandmotherly woman didn't understand my complaints.

Before the sun even rose, we were already cooking. Using those giant tortillas, we crafted what they called tlayuda—a folded tortilla loaded with plenty of shredded, mozzarella-like quesillo cheese. We grilled them over hot coals until they crisped on the outside and turned molten inside. With baskets filled to the rim, Abuela and I strolled through the waking streets, selling them for a few coins. When our baskets emptied, we restarted the process—more tortillas, more tlayudas.

After a week of this, a man dressed in dark attire arrived, armed with a military rifle. He introduced himself as Cesar and mentioned that he would be my escort for more Mexican cuisines. We journeyed deeper into Mexico. Little did I know, this man and his truck had a secondary agenda beyond my culinary endeavors. In the back of it were bodies, some alive, others dead. Each of them carrying drugs hidden in their private parts. I didn't learn this until one night a police officer who wanted a bribe to keep quiet stopped us. He demanded sex with a young American, specifically me, as payment. Luckily, Cesar—my bodyguard—wasn't at all fond of cops. When the lone arrogant police officer got handsy with me, Cesar cut off his cock and stuffed it in his mouth before leaving him for the coyotes.

From then on, my apprehension towards Cesar dissipated, transforming into a profound friendship. At our various stops, I delved into the intricacies of butchering and cleaning goats, pigs, and chickens. I mastered over 100 tamales, each with its unique flavor profile. Roasting meat over an open flame on a rotisserie spit rod became second nature, as did the art of mashing and refrying beans. And surprisingly, I discovered that there were more types of tacos than one might ever imagine. Not as many as the cars on the road, but certainly an impressive variety.

It was close to the end of my journey. Cesar had told me we'd be heading back to the states. I looked forward to my return because I had felt the effects of lack of human protein. Despite having the pick of humans in the truck's cargo area, I didn't touch them. Also, being around so many women, there were many who were ripe and piping hot. Yet, I couldn't do anything about it. Not in crowded towns and cities. Too much potential danger.

We were in the middle of nowhere in Mexico, in this small village, when I could no longer hold myself at bay. There were barely any lights, just a few torches around the village that would soon die out. My eyes caught sight of Cesar exercising his authority on some woman, pounding out his dominance.

When he came out, adjusting himself, he saw my watchful eye. "I don't know what gets you off, but if you want it, this is the place to do it. I'll even pay for you if you wanna get off. She'll do whatever for a couple hundred pesos."

I laughed. "She won't be alive by morning if I let myself go."

"Like I said, this is the place to do it. Ain't nothing that a few hundred pesos won't cover up."

He walked past me, heading toward his truck. When he did, I reached for the knife attached to his belt. He didn't stop me from taking it, though he paused and turned around. Within a few moments, I was inside this woman's tent with the knife in my hand, fileting her cunt and making that pink taco mine.

Mexican Street Tacos

Appropriately placed, here is the next recipe in our culinary journey. The Mexican street taco. I think I had mentioned before that no part of the human body goes unused; this includes the skin. I am a firm believer in not letting anything go to waste. Every part of the human body, including skin provides us with nutrients. While it is not enough to sustain us as human-eating beings, adding these little details makes the difference between being a foodie and being a junk food eater. Much like our normal counterparts, there are those who dine at fine restaurants while there are others who eat at McDonald's every day. By reminding you about the parts of the body you might toss away, I'm elevating your palate to that of a foodie.

If you take your time dismembering a body, you can slide your knife between the skin and the meat, slicing the pith apart. The pith is tendrils that keep the skin attached to the meat. Once you get a rhythm, the skin will peel off much like an orange rind. Because skin is thicker than the average tortilla, you can easily press this through a pastry roller. KitchenAid has one that works with their basic stand mixers.

Because street tacos are smaller, more like an appetizer, you want to press out the skin to a normal-sized flour tortilla. When you fry up the skin, it will shrink to the correct size for this bite-sized delight.

*For all you lovelies who like the taste of women outside of the dining room, I recommend a particular piece of skin for your taco. Per female human, you only get one of these scrumptious edibles, but you have to be ever so gentle removing it. This portion of the body is very delicate, even though it can take a beating. Go ahead. Yes, we know you want it. With a small paring knife, slice around the groin and over the pubic area. Run your finger underneath the fold and peel it away. Comes right off, especially when wet. That piece is for you.

Ingredients

2 ounces powdered ancho chile

8 garlic, cloves, unpeeled

1/2 teaspoon ground canela (or cinnamon)

1/4 teaspoon fresh black pepper

1/4 teaspoon cumin

1 teaspoon dried oregano

1/4 cup apple cider vinegar

1/4 cup of human blood

1/4 cup vegetable or olive oil, plus more for the pineapple and for the meat (if sautéing)

1 3/4 ounces achiote paste (recommended but unnecessary)

salt

8 ounces cut pineapple slices (drained)

1 tablespoon agave

1 1/2 pounds thin-sliced plump shoulder & upper arm

20 warm skin tortillas

3/4 cup chopped white onion, rinsed under cold water

1/2 cup chopped cilantro

about 1 1/2 cups salsa (your favorite variety)

Instructions

- Measure the powdered chile into a blender jar with 1 1/4 cups boiling water, blend to mix and let stand for 20 minutes.

- While the chile is rehydrating, in an ungreased skillet over medium heat, roast the garlic, turning regularly until blotchy black in places and soft.

- Cool slightly, peel and add to the blender with the chile.

- Add the cinnamon, black pepper, cumin, oregano, vinegar and two teaspoons of salt. Blend until smooth, adding the 1/4 cup of blood slowly to keep everything swimming over the blades. This should be a lovely shade of red by the time it is blended thoroughly.

- Remove 1/2 of the red adobo mixture from the blender and store for a later use*.

- Add achiote (if using), agave and oil to the blender. Finally, add one piece of pineapple to the blender and blend until very smooth. The marinade should be about as thick as ketchup.

- Spread it on both sides of the meat. If possible, cover and refrigerate for several hours or overnight.

- Heat a very large heavy skillet or cast-iron pan over medium-high heat.

- Brush or spray the pineapple with oil and sear in the skillet until nicely caramelized and warm.

- Chop into small pieces, scoop onto a baking sheet and keep warm in a very low temperature oven.

- Add a light coating of oil to the pan, then sear the meat in a single layer. While cooking the meat, chop it into small pieces and add it to the baking sheet with the pineapple.

- Mix the onions and cilantro.

- On the warm skin tortillas, build your tacos. Meat, pineapple, onions, and cilantro and a spoonful of salsa.

Notes

* Blood adobo can last for six months in a closed container in the refrigerator.

*If you happen to like a little razzle-dazzle on your tacos, and have a lot of time with your human before butchering, you can have sex with your victim and save their fluids for your own sour cream mixture. Collect and rehydrate with a bit of buttermilk. Yum!

Chapter 16

On the return from Mexico, Cesar had me exit the vehicle just before reaching the border. He instructed me to cross over via the footbridge, claiming it was safer. He explained that if I didn't see him on the other side within an hour, it meant they detained him, and I should call a specific number for my rescue. I did as he instructed. During this era, as long as you looked American, the border patrol passed you through without even checking identification. Once across, I made a call—not to that number, but to my true savior, Dianne.

She answered immediately. After being away for almost a month, hearing her voice was a relief. There had been some distance between us before I left, so I expected a lukewarm conversation. "I'm back in the states. I should be home tomorrow, barring any ride delays."

"Are you okay? Did they hurt you in any way?" she asked, concern lacing her words.

"No, everything's fine. I'm just eager to get home. I've missed—" I stopped mid-sentence.

She finished it for me. "I've really missed you."

"Same here. If something goes wrong or I'm delayed, I'll call you. Otherwise, I'll see you tomorrow?" I trailed off with a hint of uncertainty.

"Absolutely."

After the call, I disconnected and immediately spotted Cesar's truck pulling through. I dashed towards the vehicle and hopped in. The drive from the border to Albuquerque was only a day's journey, but we had to navigate many back roads to avoid patrol checkpoints scattered throughout the state.

Somewhere around three in the morning, Cesar dropped me off in front of my house. A light shone through the front window, and I assumed Dianne had left it on, not knowing exactly when I'd arrive. As soon as I put my key in the lock, the door flew open, revealing her—wide-eyed and smiling in greeting. Without a moment's hesitation, she threw her arms around me, enveloping me in a tight hug right there at the threshold of our home.

She pulled me inside and kicked the door closed. Before we had even entered the bedroom, before she even said hello, my clothes were off and so were hers. This wasn't the same lustful need that came with breathing in the scent of a woman in heat. No. This was something much deeper and more meaningful than wanting to tear the tender flesh off each other. Our mouths connected, tongues lashing within each other's mouths. Her hands found every inch of skin, dipping in and out of every hole with hungry eagerness. I hadn't expected such a welcome home, but I gladly accepted it because I missed everything about her.

Before going on this culinary excursion, I had pleaded with Colleen to let Dianne come along, but she refused, insisting I travel without my lover's distractions. It was an excruciating trip, both mentally and physically, without her by my side. But seeing this welcome, I'd endure being away just to feel her love beyond mere physical desires.

In a moment's pause, as we caught our breath, I gazed up at her eyes while resting on top of her. With a playful tone, I teased, "So, now you finally want me?"

She shook her head, inhaling my stench, which was a mix of sweat, farm animals, and sex. "No. It's that I've *always* wanted you. Cora, I wanted you even before I was allowed to have you. That's *always* been the issue and my struggle. I might not have done nice things to you if you had…"

I stopped her. If we were confessing our sins and inappropriate thoughts, I confessed mine so she didn't have to say hers. "I grew up dreaming of you. Once the urges kicked in and I realized sex felt good, I used a doll's head and wanted it to be you."

She inwardly chuckled, then slithered out from under me, ducking beneath the sheets until she found my center, spreading me open like a Thanksgiving turkey and stuffing me with a combination of her fingers and tongue. The days of imagination had ended. I ran my fingers through her feathered hair, gripping her in place while I bent my knees and let her devour the waterfall of pleasure surging from my center. When I let go, her wet face slid over my sweaty skin and met my mouth where we kissed until we fell asleep.

The phone jolted us awake around noon. It was a struggle to leave her side—I was still a teenager in love, everything so intense. But it was my boss, Colleen Marnoff, on the line.

"Are you planning to show up today, or should I assume you're disregarding our contract? I prefer certainty about my employees' whereabouts," she stated, skipping any welcome back.

My words stumbled out, "Yes, I... I mean, okay. Let me get dressed. I'll be right there."

After hanging up, I turned and practically bumped into Dianne beside me. "Colleen?"

"Seems like there's no time for rest," I muttered as I shuffled past her.

"Tell her to fuck off. You just got home."

"I don't have that luxury."

My ornery self pushed past her in the living room, down the hallway. When I had come home that night, we were fucking all the way to the bedroom, so I hadn't seen that she had decorated the other rooms. I noticed a picture frame on the nightstand as I stood at the door of my old bedroom. It held a small double bed, a dresser, and a few tables—hardly what drew my attention. Yet, there it was, the picture frame, with a silhouette of four people catching my eye. I lifted it up to get a clearer look. My heart seemed to stop as I gazed at the smiling faces of my family. My mother and father stood behind me and my sister in front of the house.

Turning with the frame in hand, I found Dianne in the doorway, leaning casually. "Where did you get this?" I asked, my voice betraying my shock.

"In the attic. Found a box tucked away—family photos, some trinkets. Figured it might make this place feel more like home," she said with a nonchalant shrug, as if it were a common gesture.

With the echoes of Colleen's angry voice still reverberating in my mind, I didn't have time for a conversation, let alone an argument. I had already resolved to never see their faces again, other than in my mind. Yet, here was a photograph placed in my childhood bedroom like a glaring taunt to bring my pain to the surface again.

"Do you feel any remorse for what you did to me and my family?"

I had thrown this in her face many times, yet I had never outright asked her if she felt sorry for her actions. We never spoke in length about it because I tried hard to move past the horrific events.

She lowered her gaze to the floor, scuffing her foot along the wooden floorboard. "No. Yes. Shit. Look, it would have happened even if I wasn't a part of it. As soon as your family walked into that diner, they had a target on their backs because that is what we did. We killed visitors to that diner and ate them. We killed. We fucked. We ate. That's what we did. That's what we do now."

There was a part of me that hated her. I would always hate her because still to this very day when I look at her, there is a memory of what she had done to my sister. "Marie was still alive when... when... pig lady cut off her head."

"Stop!" she said.

"I watched as you stripped her clothes off. One of your friends held her down so you could have your way with her." I threw the frame at her head, though she ducked.

"Stop! Cora!"

"And on that floor, you dove straight into her."

Dianne clamped her palms against her ears, trying to block out my words, but I couldn't let her shut me out. I lunged forward, grappling with her to release her hands, desperate for her to hear me out. "You killed her. You fucked her and killed her. She wasn't even 16 yet. You sick, perverted, fucking monster! I hate you!"

Eleven years of stifled sadness, depression, and rage were like a tea kettle spewing its violent steam. My fists slammed against her face, arms, and body. She didn't put up a fight at all. I needed to expel my anger. This was like an exorcism of all my pain. Tears streamed as I yelled profanities left and right, as well as threw punches, pounding her like a meat tenderizer.

When her hardened exterior softened under her own sobbing, she dropped to her knees. That did nothing to slow the assault on her. And as she weakened more, it was as if I got stronger and faster because I straddled her, slamming my fist into her face until she looked like a mangled hamburger.

Once I slowed, then stopped, she finally mumbled, her words gurgled with blood that spat out as she said, "I deserved this."

I helped her up from the ground, blood dripping from every wound on her face, her eyes barely open. I dressed her and myself, then half-carried her to the car, driving straight to Colleen's home. The guard let us in, casting a curious glance at Dianne's meatloaf-like profile.

I explained Dianne's situation in brief to Colleen, who emerged from the house, shooting a judgmental glance at Dianne's battered appearance. She promptly summoned one of her associates to handle the situation I'd caused. As they dealt with it, Colleen and I adjourned to the den to discuss my experiences in Mexico.

One detail I left out was the consumption of the village prostitute, but she seemed to have known. Obviously, my camaraderie with Cesar wasn't as strong as I'd have liked, especially when Colleen said, "Trust isn't your ally here. It's your greatest foe. You're young, and if you believe no one saw your greedy dive into a Mexican delicacy, you're more naïve than young. I've had to clean up two messes in two days–that one, and whatever's in the bathroom. If you want to remain employed, you better get your shit together."

If quitting had been an option, I would have taken it long ago. But there was a strict condition: employment was practically synonymous with survival. Over the past year, I'd seen previous employees working one day, and the next, they were on the butchering line. We ate them for dinner. Also, breakfast and lunch, too. While I might not have ended up in that night's dish, I would cease to exist.

Instead of protesting, I nodded with a sour expression. "Yes, Ma'am."

"With that off the table, let's see what you have learned. There's fresh meat in the stables." That was all she said, dismissing me with a wave.

Yes. I had sold my soul to the devil and was now obligated to keep this little succubus fed, or else. On my way to the stables, my workstation, I stopped in the room where a barely clothed man was leaning over Dianne, tending to her wounds.

"How is she?" I asked, but deep down, I directed it at her.

"She'd be better if she hadn't gotten into a fight with a lawnmower," he said. "You sure have some anger issues."

"I'd like to think that this was therapy and now I'm over it." I looked down at Dianne, towering over her. Her swollen eyelids cracked, revealing the pain in her soul. "I forgive you."

That was a lie. I would never forgive her for what she did in 1977. I still haven't even to this day. With that, I left her in his care and proceeded to the stables, where I found a young Latino boy. Not much over adulthood. Open wounds covered his body, which was beaten and bruised, with particles of dirt caked in the abrasions. His hands and legs were bound with ropes, and he had a gag in his mouth. The green in his eyes shined like emeralds, so bright that I almost needed sunglasses. Life wasn't fair. Not to me. Not to him.

On the wall was a hatchet. I glanced at it, knowing I needed to use it on him. With one swing of my arm, his head would drop next to him. His lifeless eyes, much like my sister's, would stare back at me in judgment. I couldn't bring myself to take his life, at least not yet. This kid wasn't the only person in the stables. There were others, tied up and gagged, waiting for slaughter. Honestly, I had my pick of choice meats. A truck would transport what I didn't use to the warehouse where Colleen conducted her secret buffet for cannibal women. But she had specifically directed me to this certain stable.

She wanted him. With this specimen, I would make his unique appendage into a *relleno*, stuffed with the *albondigas* and a *crema* sauce for topping. All of which I had to do myself.

But, I couldn't do it. With a yank of the hatchet, I grasped its handle and swung it down between his legs. It tore through the rope like butter, splintering the fibers in half. The same with the rope around his hands. With a shove, I pushed him out of the stable and toward the backyard. It would be a long sprint. If he made it, he'd be free. If not, we would both face slaughter.

Chili Rellenos

I am certain you would like to know if the boy made it across the property line. Well, I lived to write this book, didn't I?

One thing I learned about Colleen was that she didn't spend time in the stables. She didn't seem to appreciate the quality of her future ingredients, preferring to indulge in her hedonistic pursuits instead. Despite my own experiences with street food across the border, I still valued quality. That evening, Colleen had one demand for dinner: it didn't matter if it was a young man or a sweaty gardener, as long as her chili peppers were meaty and plump.

When the young lad made it over the gate, I waited a few minutes. Just to see if someone would bludgeon me for my treason. When no repercussions came, I sauntered to the backyard where one of the many men tending the garden worked. With a toss of my hair, a bat of my eyes, and a lift of my shirt, I lured the pudgy man into the stables, hypnotizing him with a shake of my ass. I locked us behind a steel barn door and rubbed my breasts while tugging on his belt.

He tried to touch me, but I said, "*No. Tu primero,*" telling him I wanted him to go first. When he pulled his chubby cock from his pants, I kneeled before him as if I wanted to eat him like a churro. That wasn't the case. He didn't notice the knife in my hand, so when I gripped it and gave it a firm yank, I sliced it off in one swift motion. Much faster than him, I jumped up and slammed the cock into his screaming mouth to shut him up, then sliced across his neck, cutting his jugular vein.

Of course, I needed the filling; and I needed to get rid of the body. With the boy, I would have had a little time to leave his body to cure. This guy was another story. After slicing off his balls and extracting the sausage from his mouth, I sent the rest of him through the meat grinder for hamburger. Or should we say, chorizo? And well, for that cream sauce, we will not discuss what I had to do to retrieve that. Period. We will not go there.

Ingredients

4 poblano peppers (or use New Mexican peppers, Hatch peppers, Anaheims, or others)

1 thick cock (optional if you are a lesbian; substitute with any meat)

2 testicles (optional if you are a lesbian; substitute with any meat)

2 eggs, separated

1/2 cup flour sifted

6 ounces melty cheese or equivalent of shredded cheese

Pinch of salt

Oil for frying

Instructions

- Remove the cock and testicles from the host. Slice the skin down the shaft, then carefully peel away from the member and scoop out the insides with a spoon. Set aside the skin to dry.

- Toss the inside of cock and full testicles into a meat grinder, squeezing it out into a thick coarse cut. If you choose to not use the male appendages, any coarse cut of meat will do. Then set aside.

- Blacken the pepper skins by roasting them over an open flame or using your oven broiler. Over flame, it should only take about five minutes. In the broiler, it could take 10 or more minutes.

- Remove the peppers and transfer to a paper or plastic bag and seal them up. Allow to steam and cool. This will loosen up the skin.

- Once cooled, peel off the blackened skins.

- Slice open each pepper lengthwise with one long slit, then remove the innards with a knife or spoon; just like you did the cock.

- Place one half of the cock skin in each pepper like a lining within the pepper if you are using the male meats.

- Add ground meat then cover with cheese, but do not overstuff. Make sure you can still close the pepper.

- Heat two inches of vegetable oil in a wide pot to 375 degrees. Do not let the oil boil. If you do not have a thermometer, test the oil with a tiny drop of flour. It will immediately sizzle up.

- Separate the egg yolks from the whites and add the egg whites into a large bowl. Beat the egg whites until they fluff up and form stiff peaks, about five minutes. An electric eggbeater is ideal. Gently stir in egg yolks.

- Add flour to a separate bowl with a bit of salt. Dip the stuffed peppers into the flour to coat them, then dip them into the egg batter to coat them completely.

- Fry each pepper for about two to three minutes on each side, or until they are a golden brown.

- Remove the peppers and set them onto a paper-towel-lined plate to drain excess oil.

- Serve with your favorite salsa or cream sauce.

Chapter 17

Over the next year, Colleen sent me to faraway lands. In Brazil, I mastered Feijoada, a rich stew blending black beans with various cuts of pork, tomatoes, cabbage, and carrots, for a well-rounded flavor profile.

My next stop was in Curaçao, where a local chef shared the recipe for papaya stobá, a stew made with salted meat and pig tail. Interestingly, during this trip, the man who taught me this dish had a wife who had recently contracted the same cannibal infection, and he confided this information to me. Instead of using salted meat and pigtail, he actually used the lining of rectums of people he killed for her. Very salty indeed.

From there, I journeyed to Honduras, where I learned to prepare dishes using innards like tripe, the stomach lining used in a dish called soupa de mondongo.

Each time I returned from a country, Dianne greeted me at the door with an erotic dance that led us into the bedroom. Despite enjoying the travel and learning experiences, coming home meant facing Colleen's overly critical palate. It seemed unlikely that she had ever been to these countries or knew the authentic taste of these dishes. Her increasingly harsh criticism of my cooking of these foreign cuisines grew bothersome.

It felt less like working for someone keen on savoring food and more like being under the command of a drill sergeant. I discovered an array of new flavors, and back home, I shared these experiences with Dianne, who appreciated them. But it seemed only she did. Not that Colleen despised my efforts; she simply insisted they lacked flavor, always asking for more. This just would not cut it for me, especially when I grew tired of being a murderer.

Cannibalism and murder seem to go hand in hand, right? Obviously, if you are a cannibal, you eat people. We do not find the nutrients we need in rotted or decomposed bodies. For the meat to remain viable, it needs to be cut and cleaned within a few days; otherwise, it loses the potency of the chemical compounds essential for our survival. Freezing the meat is one method, but there's another. If the body stays warm after death, the vitamins and minerals remain active. I learned about this when Colleen sent me to Europe, specifically Poland.

They took me to a human butchery, where they explained the curing process to me. In their hot house, which maintained a temperature of 76 degrees, they warmed slabs of salt with curing bodies hanging from the rafters. They had already skinned these bodies and removed most of their organs. The impurities from the salt, particularly those containing potassium nitrates, were used to impart a distinct flavor that was highly sought after. This compound, commonly known as saltpeter, was a fundamental ingredient in gunpowder, an invention attributed to the Chinese thousands of years ago.

A freezer could only hold so much food. With this new knowledge, I could keep a larger supply of meat on a rotation, which meant killing less often. Therefore, we could bring in a truckload of viable sources of protein, do one mass slaughter, then house their bodies in a low-heat sauna until we needed them.

While in Poland, the idea came to me when I spent the week working in the curing center. This disease had spread like a pandemic. Women turning into cannibals received coverage on the evening news in Poland. Instead of eradicating or finding a cure for the disease, Poland fed it with underground meat markets. Unlike Colleen's way of feeding the zoo creatures, this country had solved their homeless problem by rounding up the vagrants and providing fresh carnage for home usage. This lessened the population while keeping feral bitches from terrorizing the major cities by going on killing sprees.

What if Dianne and I could do something like this? I pondered as I hung a carcass on a meat hook at one of their markets. We could treat it like a deli of sorts. Slices of meat or larger cuts. Even provide ground beef for those who didn't have a grinder at home. Smoke them. Maybe even make sausage-like links.

When I returned home, I shared the idea with Dianne. She declared I was officially crazy and had lost my mind while pointing out the challenges of finding a location for such a facility and the difficulties in keeping such a business venture a secret. Plus, she reminded me that butchering people wasn't my forte.

What I didn't confide in Dianne was my growing desperation to break free from Colleen's hold. I had signed my name in blood and sold my soul. Now I despise everything about her.

One particular evening, Colleen had a large get together—more like a harem of men over for her delight. I think there were over 20 different guys, all for one woman. When I said that our sex drives worked overtime, this was no joke. Were it not for the obligation of leaving my house for work, Dianne and I would probably never leave the bedroom. We fucked more than we ate. Colleen was no exception. Her insatiable appetite for dick was like an alcoholic on a binge.

During that evening, the house chef prepared Chinese cuisine for these robust young men. However, my attempt at replicating the dish failed to satisfy even my taste buds. It lacked flavor, was too thin, and the seasoning didn't blend well. This led me to my next destination: China.

In contrast to my other work trips, China felt more like a rejuvenating getaway. While I grappled daily with perfecting hand-pulled noodles and Beggar's chicken to meet the standards of a seasoned Chinese expert, I also dedicated hours to practicing Xi-Sui-Jing-Qi-Gong, a form of meditation from the Song Shan Mountains. This sacred exercise regimen, rooted in traditional Shaolin medicine, aimed to strengthen bones, purify bone marrow, and enhance blood quality. Comprising 12 individual exercises, we performed these routines in a seated position, fostering recovery for both body and soul.

Initially, my restless nature resisted the idea of turning inward to my physical sensations. It wasn't until Mr. Miyagi, or rather, the man I initially referred to as Mr. Miyagi for the sake of familiarity, explained that there was a demon within me—the Qiongqi. I couldn't comprehend how he perceived this creature within my soul, but he did.

In Chinese mythology, Qiongqi is one of the four malevolent creatures banished by the gods. Alongside Hundun, Taowu, and Taotie, Qiongqi embodies deviousness and resembles a winged tiger that incites conflict, consumes humans, and commits many malicious acts.

"You must purify yourself. Rid your mind of the beast dwelling within you. The Qiongqi is undeniably powerful, but you must be stronger, lest it consumes those of noble spirit," Fu Lao advised as I worked on stretching noodle dough in the kitchen of his restaurant.

"I am not sure this beast is not in my head. It's very real, and is eating me from the inside," I responded.

Fu Lao's daughter, Mey, stood beside me as I worked the dough every day in the workshop. She'd come in regularly and stayed by my side, silently observing as I put in the hours. After work, we'd step into the garden for our meditation, where she'd sit cross-legged on my mat beside me. Her peculiar fascination with me struck me as odd; Mey rarely left the residence for school or play. So, in the evenings when Fu Lao managed his business, I'd read to Mey from a collection of classic English tales.

One night, after we finished our reading session, Mey, who didn't speak English, uttered something to me in Chinese. I didn't understand her words, but she drew a picture of the Qiongqi and pointed at me. It was clear she knew something, too.

But since she didn't speak English, I confessed my worries to her. "I know, I eat people. There is something wrong with me because this should not be my life. It wasn't my destiny to transform into a wolf-person who feasts on humans. I mean, you are lucky because you are only a child, and I can't eat children, but there really is something inside of me that is dark and evil, and I don't know how to get rid of it."

There must have been some truth to the creature's existence if more than one person could sense the beast within me. China and its culture were very calm, unlike back home, where there was traffic, crime, and violence. Maybe it was because I wasn't in a large city, but they just seemed to have their shit together. In this small town outside of Beijing, the people weren't in a hurry. They took time to breathe, to escape, to just be one with the land.

Because of this, on the next day after our meditation, I asked, "How do I cleanse myself to get rid of the Qiongqi?"

Fu Lao didn't answer my question, leaving me perplexed and hanging, hoping for some magic banishing method to extract the demon that made me want to eat women, and not in a good way. When we arrived at his home, he motioned for me to follow him, which I did, leading to a room filled with bottles and jars, almost as if he were a witch doctor who conjured up potions in his spare time.

From the door, I watched as he pondered the glass jars that bore labels with dark slashes—paint strokes of a thick fountain pen that formed words in a language I didn't understand. He petted his long gray beard, gripping it so that it made a point at his chest. The mumbled words were in his native tongue as he pulled a bottle of this and a jar of that.

After gathering various ingredients, he took all of them to a table and sat in front of it. Again, he motioned for me to join him, where he started his mixture. "*He huan pi*, happy bark. It calms the unrested. Dang shen, codonopsis root for your belly."

When he opened the next jar, a waft of death snaked through the room, as if a zombie rose like a genie from a bottle. Maybe the zombie killed the genie, but whatever it was, it stunk.

"What the hell? Smells like a massive fart explosion," I said in my very teenage verbiage.

He didn't laugh. "Rafflesia arnoldii, stem of the corpse flower."

There was one other bottle he had with him. I asked, "What's that one?"

"This is what will kill you and the Qiongqi. *Fùzǐ de gēn hé kuàijīng*. Roots and tubers of monkshood. Poison to bring death to the enemy."

What? My eyes widened as I verbalized what was in my head at that moment. I pulled the bottle to me, giving it a sniff. A little of it wafted up, tickling my nose. I batted the air. "What the hell? You're gonna kill me with that fuzzy stuff?"

In his stone mortar and pestle, he crushed it together, then handed it to me. "Smell. It's now very sweet."

I did. Somehow, the mingling of scents changed death into life. Floral notes as if waking up in a field of flowers.

We brewed hot tea, and he sprinkled some of the mixture into the warmth of my cup. Then on his zen patio, we sat cross-legged on mats.

"Once the Qiongqi takes hold, you must die and rebirth yourself. Free of sin. Free from pain," Fu said.

"What you're saying is that this will kill me? And you want me to drink it?"

"No, not me, you. You want to cleanse yourself; here is the cleanse. I want nothing. You do," he replied.

This was what I asked for: his help. For over 2,000 years, Chinese healers have used herbal powders and tinctures. However, these home remedies were unregulated, and they frequently made people sick rather than curing them. I had a choice: I could believe in 2,000 years of folklore and possibly die forever, or I could remain a cannibal for the rest of my life.

Chinese Meaty Noodles

Chinese noodles are probably one of the easiest recipes, but also one of the hardest to get consistent. With only four ingredients, it is pretty simple. If you would like to use your KitchenAid mixer and its pasta attachments, that is perfectly acceptable. I still, to this day, do the work by hand.

Because most of the flavor comes from the seasonings, it is unnecessary to use a person of Chinese descent for this meal. There is no difference in the taste of this meal. However, if you did, I would recommend slicing from the calf. I am bemused because, for some strange reason, their lower half has a stronger salt flavor. With the many Asians I have eaten in my life, each of them had salty meat along their leg bones.

Ingredients

Noodles

2 cups all purpose flour

1 teaspoon of salt

2/3 cups warm water

1/4 cup vegetable oil

Instructions

- In a sizable bowl, incorporate flour and salt and then combine thoroughly. Pour in warm water, and mix with a chopstick until flakey. Knead until it forms into a ball, cover, and let it rest for 10 minutes.

- After 10-15 minutes, knead until smooth. Once the dough is smooth, roll it out and cut it into eight pieces.

- Roll those eight pieces into balls.

- In a bowl, add in 1/4 cup of oil. Add in all the pieces and coat with oil. Cover and let it rest for one hour or more. In China, we let these sit overnight in the oil. Room temperature is fine.

- After said time, roll out the dough. Pull on both ends, and hit the dough against the countertop to stretch. Keep hitting until about 1/2 centimeter in thickness. Break it apart where you made a dent earlier to form into two long pieces of noodle.

- With a dough cutter, indent and separate into strips about half an inch.

- Again, slowly pull those into longer noodles.

- Cook the noodles in hot water for three to four minutes, drain and enjoy!

Meat dish
Ingredients
1 serving of noodles of your choice
1/3 cucumber, cut into match-sized sticks
1/4 pound of meat slices cut into squares about 1/2 inch thick
1/4 cup diced onion
2 dried shiitake mushrooms, rehydrated and diced
1 tablespoon diced ginger
2 tablespoons chopped green onion
2 tablespoons oil

For the sauce:
3 tablespoons soybean paste
2 tablespoons sweet bean sauce
2 tablespoons cooking wine (preferred is Shaoxing)
3-4 tablespoons water
1/4 teaspoon sugar

Instructions

- Whisk soybean paste, sweet bean paste, cooking wine, water, and sugar in a container in advance and set aside for later use.

- Heat a pan over medium-low heat, add oil and stir in mushroom, onion, ginger, and green onion; stir-fry for three to four minutes until the onion turns translucent.

- Add the meat slices into the pan, stir-fry for another five minutes until the beef has turned a grayish color.

- Pour in the sauce, stir and mix well with the ingredients and simmer for about two to three minutes on low heat.

- Pour the meat and sauce onto the noodles and top with cucumber to serve.

Chapter 18

When I returned from the East, Dianne welcomed me home, but this time, it felt different. I don't know if it was because I had finally learned to center myself or because I could play God. In my hands (actually my jeans' front pocket, in a little bottle), I held the ancient Chinese secret, and it wasn't Calgon. When Fu Lao promised to purify me of my transgressions, I erroneously assumed it encompassed my attraction towards women. Or one woman. Dianne. As much as I wanted to be free from the Qiongqi, or this flesh-eating bacteria inside me, I didn't want to lose the one thing that had gotten me through growing up a cannibal: my love for this woman. And while I didn't want to lose the feeling inside me, I felt some God complex and wanted to cure Dianne more than myself.

Instead of drinking the concoction in China, I returned home with the poisoned spice blend with the plan to serve it up to Dianne, whether she liked it or not.

At the front door, again, she scooped me up in one giant swoop and carried me into the bedroom. My nose tickled as she hurried down the hall, dropped me on the bed, and began tearing at my clothes as if they were a hindrance to her need. At first, I laughed, but her nails clawed my skin, digging into the flesh as if they were razor blades. The red in her eyes told me that there was fresh meat in the house. This was against the rules. As a chef, I provided her with enough meals so she didn't need to stalk prey. I had turned this scavenger into an almost proper member of society, yet...

I pushed her off of me and as I did, her nail clipped me. The skin separated and beads of red liquid seeped out like dew on a blade of grass. Her eyes widened, drool foaming at the side of her mouth.

Slowly, I shifted away from her as she tried to retreat also, but I could tell that was a struggle. It wasn't just that kiss of blood upon my breast that summoned her primal hunger; it was the fact that I was on my period. In the past, we never cared about that because blood was a part of our life, but the blood I dripped from my sex was the reason for Dianne's rage. No. It wasn't fresh meat in the house. It was me.

"Dianne, stop. Don't do this!" I said as I pulled myself from the bed. I stood on one side while she was on the other, forming an intricate dance of cat and mouse.

She licked her lips, knowing there was a problem. "What the hell? I can smell you. You're cured?"

"I am not. I'm me. The same Cora you love, not to eat. Something's the matter with you."

"It's you."

"No!" I screamed at her as she stalked closer to me. I had no escape route as I found myself backed into the corner of our room. The room we shared as lovers, and it looked like our bed would become my deathbed. There were two things we always kept near us: one was a snack to stop the cravings when out in public.

When Dianne lunged at me, her jaw opened like a great white shark, leaping from the ocean. She caught my hand in her mouth, tearing the skin as I jumped over the bed, making a dive for the second thing that we also had in this bedroom. A gun. As fast as I could, I opened the drawer and grasped the gun, pointing it at her. She paused for a moment, standing on top of the bed, as my mangled hand shook with the gun aimed directly at her head. The skin hung from my muscles as she had torn most of it away in that clench. The pain was unrelenting as blood dripped over the grip of the gun.

I finally knew exactly how my sister felt, being eaten by this woman. And as if some morbid curiosity came over me, I wanted her to do it. I wanted to feel her teeth sink into my flesh, into my cunt, swallow me whole. Part of me wanted to be inside her, not just fucking her, but being the food to give this woman life. I thought that if she ate me, I'd always be a part of her. And so I lowered the gun.

"What are you doing?" Dianne said, her feet digging into the sheets as if readying herself to pounce like a hungry lioness.

"You need to eat me." I tossed the gun to the ground and lowered myself to it. "Start with my sex. Please!"

My shirtless body rested on the ground. I wasn't even tense, because I had made peace with my death. While I didn't understand how this metamorphosis happened, it had. Fu Lao had cured me in China, and I walked straight into the lion's den wearing a giant hunk of red, moist meat around my neck.

"I don't want to do that," Dianne said, though she didn't back down. Her eyes still glowed with fire, and she had a strain in her voice. This was killing her, just as it was me.

"If I would have stayed with you, back then, you would have done this to me when I became a woman. Am I right?" I said, as I leaned on my elbows, looking at her and the pain on her face.

She nodded a slow bob. "Yes. And I don't like admitting that."

"Would you have torn it away like you did to my sister?" I asked.

"No." She inched forward. "I would have wanted to savor you. To taste the fear on your skin."

While I might not have shown it, I feared the unknown. The sweat that had pooled at the base of my back was from that. It had also pooled between my thighs. My inner muscles vibrated, pulsating my veins with adrenaline. This was fear.

"Show me," I said. "I'm giving you the chance to do what you've always wanted. Savor me."

I dropped my head back and let her move on top of me. This would be our last dance. Her extra wet tongue dripped with saliva as it slid over my breast, sucking and tugging at my nipple and giving extra attention to where her nail had tenderized my skin. It was as if her powerful muscle could spread the wound, opening it so she could use it as another cunt, lapping it up and down in an erotic sawing motion. With my hands on her head, I guided her downward. My need grew because I wanted her face buried in the blazing sauna of my sex. When she reached my groin, she inhaled so deep that I thought her lungs would burst. Her hands ran over my jeans, but she gave pause. Something caught her attention. Her hand dug into my pocket and pulled the bottle of poisonous spice blend from it.

She shook the small vine of powder. That's when I realized. I hadn't drunk the monkshood but inhaled it. That night, I slept so peacefully after the monkshood's dust particles coated the inside of my nostrils. More like I was dead to the world and woke up invigorated with a new sense of life. Funny how I walked through the airport and felt no urge. Because of my forced self-control, I thought little of it. Although my death had arrived in the middle of the night without my knowledge, my subsequent rebirth had purged me of any inclination to indulge in the consumption of ripe flesh.

I took the little bottle from her hand and allowed Dianne to continue, letting her pull off my jeans and my underwear. Her fingers stiffened and her nails extended like violent claws. They pressed into my skin as if it were an orange rind to be torn away from the juiciness of my fruit. My legs spread with an open invitation for her to kill me. She licked up my leg; her tongue bathing me in drool with a scratchiness to her taste buds.

At first, she lapped at the blood that had pooled between the folds, groaning like she had just tasted the most delectable dessert. Her tongue hit my clit. Just like that, I shuddered and melted into her face. Her mouth wrapped around that engorged hunk of womanly flesh and, just as her teeth sank into the ripest grapefruit, I came.

My orgasm was so hard I could feel the warmth of my secretions dripping between my legs. The scream was pleasure mixed with excruciating pain. So much that the little bottle of poison clenched in my hand broke, crushing sharp, jagged pieces of glass into my palm. The powdery substance landed on me, on her, and all over the bed. It might have been my imagination, but it was as if all the Chinese Gods circled around us in a cloud of dust, attacking the Qiongqi inside Dianne.

She lifted her head from my snatch. Her blood-covered mouth opened wide, and a giant howl of pain ripped from her gut. I swear the winged tiger flew out of her mouth as she violently vomited over me. Red bile projected forward, spewing out with such force, it coated the walls as if someone tossed a pail of paint everywhere. Kicking away, I pinned myself against the wall with nowhere else to go. It came at me, relentlessly, covering me with the lifetime of sins expelling from her.

And then it stopped. Her body slumped to the floor, unmoving, not breathing. I pulled my body away from the wall, which dripped with what looked like hot spaghetti sauce. Chunks of meat particles fell from me as I reached for Dianne's limp body and felt for a pulse. There was none. Despite the pain I was in and the bleeding from my sex that wasn't part of some monthly breeding ritual, I draped my body over hers, holding her and praying that she would wake up from this deadly sleep.

Multi-use Pasta Sauce

I am sure you are wondering what happened to Dianne. You will need to wait until I give you the recipe for the hot spaghetti sauce that covered me on the floor. Make a woman vomit after she has eaten. And done.

If only it were that simple. I am confident that you have no desire to spoil your noodles with repulsive projectile vomit. But for this recipe, we will use the drained blood from your human victim. If you are a person who likes sugar in their spaghetti sauce, you will want the blood from a woman. It will already be sweet enough and will not need extra sugar added. For those purists, male blood is perfect. And for me, this is the only time I might seek a male victim if I want a great Italian pasta sauce.

If you are holding a live human hostage and letting the adrenaline course through their veins, it is wise to stick a container under the body when you kill them. I like to use a five-gallon plastic paint bucket for the job. When you slice open their jugular vein, it will run down the body from the neck, and you want to catch as much of that as possible. Most of the time, your victim will also urinate themselves at the same time. This is just fine, and honestly, you probably want that. Natural salt is much better than adding it at the end. Urine will provide that saltiness.

A 150-180 pound body contains approximately one and a half gallons of blood. Using the plastic bucket makes it easy to carry. If you are into canning and jarring, this is the perfect time to divide up the blood into usable sizes. Mason jars are perfect for this. You can store it in the refrigerator for six months before it loses its effectiveness. Another use for blood would be for morning smoothies. Pour over crushed ice and flavor with fruit. Or add some vodka with some Tabasco and Worcestershire sauce, and you'll have a Bloody Mary.

Now, on with the pasta sauce...

Ingredients

1/3 cup good quality extra virgin olive oil

Pinch of red pepper flakes

4 crushed garlic cloves

3/4 cup chopped onion (optional)

1 teaspoon fresh chopped oregano, divided, or 1/2 teaspoon dried

1 tablespoon chopped fresh basil, divided, or 1/2 tablespoon dried

1 teaspoon fresh chopped mint, divided

1/4 teaspoon freshly ground black pepper

28 ounces human blood

1/4 cup freshly grated Parmigiano Reggiano cheese

2 tablespoons unsalted butter

Instructions

- In a large heavy-bottomed pot with a lid, pour in olive oil and add red pepper flakes, garlic, onion, most of the oregano, basil, and mint (save a little of each for the end), and pepper.

- Turn on the burner and slowly bring up to hot. When the onions and garlic cook, stir and heat for five minutes.

- Remove the pot from the burner and place a heat diffuser over the burner. Place the pot over the heat diffuser and add the blood. Turn the burner to medium-high and stir until they boil. Then reduce to simmer, partially cover and simmer 90 minutes.

- After 90 minutes, remove from heat and add the reserved herbs.

- Add the butter to round out the flavors and stir.

Notes

The spices in this pasta sauce will infuse more flavor the longer it sits. It's recommended to let your sauce rest for at least 24 hours before serving.

Chapter 19

Four celestial animals came to me after I murdered Dianne using poisonous dust powder. The Azure dragon grew from the particles, dispelling evil and negative energies from me, from Dianne, and from the house. The vermilion bird with a chicken's head, snake's neck, swallow's chin, and fish's tail flew up from those same ashes and plucked the five-colored feathers from its body, which fluttered over Dianne's dead soul. A white tiger leaped through the open bedroom door and licked the blood from Dianne's face, cleaning her so I could admire her one last time.

And last, a black turtle scooted across the carpet toward us and looked up at me with an inquisitive face. I don't know why I spoke to this creature, but I asked, "Xuanwu, will my love stay dead?"

And just as my question ended with that punctuated word, a snake slithered out from his body. "For as long as it takes for the shé to squeeze life into her."

I jerked up, flying nearly out of my skin as this long black snake continued to unwind from the tortoise's shell and wrapped its body around Dianne, cocooning every inch of her body. It took almost an hour for the snake to mummify Dianne. As soon as all of its long noodle shape had come out of the shell, I could no longer see any part of my love's body. It was as if someone had pumped air into the reptile; its body expanded, then shed its skin as it unraveled.

With the bird sitting on my bloody shoulder, I watched as the snake slipped back into the turtle's shell. Each of the four creatures blessed the room as they left me with my still-dead lover. My eyes closed and when I pressed them tight, a tear tracked a clean river over my cheek. The water droplet fell onto Dianne's cheek, dripped down to her lips, and seeped into her mouth. Her breath cut through the silence as it drew into her lungs, inflating them with life.

Dianne lived. Just as I had. And it cured her. She could no longer smell me. The desire to kill me had vanished. The need to consume flesh—any flesh—had gone away. And so had the urge to love me.

As we sat there looking at each other, I sensed she wanted to leave. We said nothing to each other as she showered, dressed, and finally left the house. No kiss goodbye. No words to say she'd see me later. Nothing but sadness in her eyes.

I waited for her to return, but she never did. After I had concluded that I'd never see Dianne again, I left the house, for the first time, feeling vulnerable. Before, my disease made me feel invincible, like nothing and no one could harm me. Now that I no longer had the disease squirming in me like a belly full of maggots, this inherent sense of worry had me looking over my shoulder the entire time as I traveled to Colleen's house.

She knew the moment I rang the doorbell that I was in danger. From her, from the cannibal community.

"How are you not infected?" she asked. "I can smell your period."

"A very ancient Chinese secret. And if you promise not to kill me and eat me, I can get it for you. Possibly for everyone," I said to her, shaking because to her, my open wounds and bleeding sex were like a hot bowl of soup on a cold winter's day.

Her mouth salivated just by my presence. "Come in. Let's talk. Where is your guardian?" She held the door open for me to enter.

The mansion felt like an alligator pit, and I could almost hear the jaws snapping shut with each cautious step. "She's gone. Cured too, and well… she left me."

Over the course of the next hour, I explained my trip to China and how Fu Lao explained the Qiongqi, or human-eater, had invaded our bodies and wreaked havoc on the female sinners of our world. Of course, Colleen laughed. I'm sure you are laughing with her. But the proof of his cure had worked twice. With her help, I could return to China and Fu Lao to create and send this spice blend to the states—to her—where she could distribute it amongst the community. If we could cure Albuquerque, more could follow.

We made one more agreement. She would take my memoir, the manuscript of my life, and have it published for those people who had yet to be cured. If they still needed meat, I'd rather they eat well and healthy than bottom-feed like a tilapia. On the condition that she come back to life after ingesting the death dust, she agreed to this. With that, she sent me back to China.

Shortly after I left China the first time, Fu Lao passed away. When I arrived at his house, his daughter Mey, who spoke perfect English to me, broke the news. First, I was astonished that she could speak my language, which meant she knew my secret and understood my confession. Second, it devastated me because it was his potion that I needed to learn and mass-produce. With his death, the entire trip was a waste. When I explained this to Mey, she grabbed my wrist and dragged me into Fu Lao's laboratory, where her older brother had taken over the family business.

Taking all the ingredients I remembered, we made a new version of the magical cure-all and shipped it off to Colleen with a note that explained this may no longer work and a phone number of where she could call if she didn't die. Every time that phone rang, I rushed to it, hoping to hear her voice. Finally, I did. I had cured Colleen. And so I began writing this memoir.

A year had passed since I killed Dianne. A day that I wished never had happened. But it did. As I sat on my mountaintop, I looked out at the vast land around me, and I was at peace. Lush trees filled the magnificent steep canyons, and the cliffside roads led to charming little villages similar to the one where I lived. I won't say where in the 3.7 million square miles of China I lived, and still do, because I wish to remain anonymous in my new life.

In my life, I have done many things I am not proud of, such as killing people, dismembering bodies, cooking them up, and even destroying families. But there are so many good things I have accomplished, such as finding a cure. While western medicine will always be about making money and keeping people just ill enough for more medicine, doctors still were not willing to take a chance on Colleen's proven cure, because the government would have to admit there was a true outbreak of cannibalism. This they would never do. Instead, they slapped a warning label on movies and television shows that stated it is unsafe to eat humans. Wow! As if that wasn't common sense. Although some communities see it as a fetish, few people purposely do it for fun.

Since Colleen's cure, we have been steadily making this unique spice blend, shipping it to the states, and distributing it through an underground network. Supplies are not plentiful because of the limited availability of Rafflesia arnoldii, the corpse flower. It has made progress slow. While these bottles of spice will cure the ailments, it is not a forever fix. You can become reinfected.

This I know from experience because after about a year of being in China, there was a knock on the Laos' door. Mey rose from the floor and opened the door to Dianne standing on the opposite side. She had visited Colleen and begged her to disclose my location. With Colleen's help, Dianne had traveled clear across the world to reunite with me.

"What are you doing here?" I asked, because I hadn't expected to ever see her again.

Still not being a woman of many words, she failed to answer me until I joined her outside. With the door closed against from prying eyes and ears, she said to me, "I want to love you again."

"I think you being here says you already do," I said, shaking my head with a chuckle.

"That might be true, but it's not the same. I can't get you out of my mind. Cora, I want to want you. I want to crave you so bad that it hurts. When I look at you, I need to feel that energy again."

"Then do it. I'm right here."

She paced. Then, as if a magnet drew her attention back to me, she twisted around, offering a package to me. "Without this, I have no feelings. I'm dead inside. Lost. As much as I want to be here with you, I need more."

I knew exactly what was in the bag. It was human meat. Fresh meat. Think of it as a junkie holding a needle and contemplating using again. So many emotions, feelings, desires, and sins came with that hunk of meat. The thought of it had crossed my mind while being away because the lingering taste remained. Imagining the familiar comfort of warm blood on my tongue was all too powerful. Diets fail for this reason. People remember the taste of chocolate cake. Denying themselves a fix makes them want that cake even more. This was that time. Dianne tested my willpower.

"You haven't eaten it? Even nibbled?" I asked.

"No. Do this with me. Let's go back to our previous life. I hate this world because I am a monster, like you said. I've done things I'm not proud of since I left. But with this, I can be with you again. I need that memory, Cora. Do you understand what I am saying?"

I reached out for her, but she pressed the bag into my hand. I knew what she meant. Without the Qiongqi inside us, we were just two women who existed on a plane full of mundane lifeless souls. With this drug—this human addictive body killer—I became a vision of predatory sin, which Dianne wanted to live. Oddly, I wanted to be that person too–to throw away all my newfound peace for the passion we once shared, even if she saw me as a child.

With that, I unwrapped the wet flesh and held it up to my mouth. Without Dianne, my life had been boring. There were no desires. I felt no love for another, and even though I tried to date and attempted to connect with others, no one could take Dianne's place. I wanted Dianne as much as she wanted me. We just needed that push to bring us back together. To get it, I ran my tongue over the tender tissue, its juices sizzling on my tongue like hot coals. As soon as I took a large bite from it, Dianne grabbed it from me and consumed the rest of it, like a kid at a pie-eating competition.

And then we waited. The infection inside me and her happened within a few days. It magically transported us back to Hell Kitchen, where we first met. Me loving Farrah, and her savoring that first memory of me. We reverted to our cannibalistic state and fed on the bodies of wanderers who had already been forgotten. We are very much in love and happy because we each have our soulmate. We have each other.

Mey and her brother are continuing my mission to cure the world one bottle at a time. So, as I sit in the China mountains, loving my Farrah, I write this final recipe. Because, if you have made it through to the end of this book and cooked all the recipes as instructed, you are a cannibal, too. Now, if you wish to cure yourself and go back to the ordinary life you once lived... turn the page. If you would like to remain a human-eating rabid creature, then I applaud you and direct you back to the beginning of the book and let's "master the art of female cookery" once more.

The Cure

Because you are here, you want to be cured. Knowing that all of your sex drive and all of your insatiable desires will be gone, if you choose to go through with the death of your life and soul just to be reborn into a boring homosapien, this is how you do it.

#killtheqiongqi

This is it. Post this hashtag on any social media account. The rebellion will reach out and send you this magical spice blend for free. It doesn't take much to exorcize the Qiongqi from your body. Trust me, it will hurt like a motherfucker.

If afterward, you hate yourself for doing it... there are two options for you: kill yourself or eat another human.

The choice is yours. I made mine, and I've never been happier.

FIN

Thank you for reading
Mastering The Art of Female Cookery

I hope you enjoyed this book. If you did, please take a moment to leave a review on either Amazon or Goodreads. Reviews are the lifeline of an author, even if just a rating.

It's the easiest and quickest way to support indie authors.

Cyan LeBlanc

Sapphic writer, Cyan LeBlanc has been writing since about 2008, starting in fanfiction. They have journeyed into the world of lesfic and is delighted to share upcoming works with women loving women fans. A multi-genre writer, Cyan focuses on Sapphic characters in romance, horror, thriller, and more.

Originally from California, Cyan currently resides in Houston, Texas where they are a florist by day and Sapphic writer by night.

Signup for the author's newsletter at www.posiesandpeacocks.com

Undertaker Books
www.undertakerbooks.com

If you are a fan of horror stories and tales, you'll want to follow Undertaker Books.

We're bringing you stories to take to your grave.
SIGN UP FOR OUR NEWSLETTER ONLINE

Made in the USA
Columbia, SC
07 June 2025